THE MONTERANT AFFAIR

THE MONTERANT AFFAIR

by

RICHARD GRAYSON

ST. MARTIN'S PRESS
NEW YORK

Library of Congress Cataloging in Publication Data

Grindal, Richard.
 The Monterant affair.

 I. Title.
PR6057.R55M6   1980   823′.914   80-51382
ISBN 0-312-54665-3

THE MONTERANT AFFAIR

I

THE AUDIENCE IN the Théâtre du Châtelet sat silent and absorbed as they watched the closing moments of *La Dame aux Camélias*. On the stage the courtesan, Marguerite, was dying of consumption in front of her lover, Armand Duval. Most of the people in the theatre had seen the play before, some many times, but the ending seldom failed to move them.

Sophie Monterant, the actress playing Marguerite, was declaiming her final lines. Not even the exaggerated pallor of a consumptive's make-up could conceal her striking beauty.

'Armand, give me your hand. . . . I can assure you it isn't hard to die.'

A few seconds later, gently and without histrionics, Marguerite died, leaving Armand distraught with anguish, and it was one of the minor characters, Marguerite's friend Nichette, who ended the play with a spoken epitaph.

'Sleep in peace, Marguerite. You will be forgiven much because you loved so much.'

The curtain was lowered slowly and after a long moment of emotional silence, the theatre erupted with tumultuous applause. To almost hysterical cheering the curtain calls began, with the leading actress modestly acknowledging the many flowers that were carried up on to the stage.

Gautier and Duthrey had been sitting by an aisle and were able, while the ovation still continued, to leave their seats and make their way out of the theatre to a line of fiacres which stood waiting on the corner of Rue de Rivoli. They had agreed to dine after the theatre at the Cloiserie des Lilas and the fiacre took them towards the Ile de la Cité and the Left Bank beyond.

'That was the first time you'd seen Sophie Monterant, wasn't it?' Duthrey asked Gautier. 'What did you think of her?'

'I was impressed. She has style, that one.'

'Style certainly. And courage as well.'

'You mean because she dared to appear in a play which the great Sarah believes to be hers by divine right?'

'Yes, and in the Châtelet, just across the road from the Théâtre Sarah-Bernhardt.'

'Perhaps she's one of those people who likes to thumb a nose at royalty.'

Sarah Bernhardt was one of the most widely known and admired actresses in the world. She had played Marguerite scores of times in Paris as well as in most of the capitals in Europe and it had been one of the most popular rôles in the repertoires of her great tours of the United States. Although she was now not far short of sixty, Sarah could still play the parts of young women with enough conviction to fill a theatre.

'I prefer Monterant's acting to that of Bernhardt,' Gautier remarked. 'She's more realistic. Bernhardt's ranting and grimaces are too exaggerated for my liking.'

Duthrey laughed. 'So you too have been seduced by the modern heretics?'

'What heretics?'

'The new realists; playwrights who put some bestial, oafish character on the stage, make him shout "Merde" a couple of times and think they are giving us immortal drama.'

This time Gautier laughed. 'I think you're the one who has been seduced—by the theatre. Why this sudden interest in the stage? Is *Figaro* making you its dramatic critic?'

'Heaven forbid! No, it's just that I have to write an article on Sophie Monterant, not so much on her career, you understand, but on the woman. I spent three hours talking to her in her apartment the other day. But how can one write about an actress without first watching her act?'

'How did you find her as a person?'

'Seductive, full of charm and vitality, but tough.'

'Didn't she cause some great scandal a year or two ago?'

'Yes. She married the famous English actor, James Henry,

walked out on the marriage after a few weeks and then had the temerity to get a divorce.'

Their fiacre was passing the Palais de Justice. To their left the twin towers of Notre Dame stood watching over the moonlit city, symbols of tranquillity. And yet, Gautier reflected, only a short distance away his colleagues on night duty at Sûreté headquarters would be involved in the turbulent real-life drama of Paris after dark: robberies in the wealthy houses on Avenue du Bois, a knifing in Place Pigalle, perhaps a student riot in Montparnasse.

As usual the Cloiserie des Lilas was crowded. Long recognized as a meeting-place for writers and poets, it was now becoming popular with artists, many of whom were drifting away from the cafés and restaurants of Montmartre to escape the extravagant behaviour and excesses of the misfits and foreign eccentrics who were flocking to the Butte, drawn by its growing reputation as the spiritual home of bohemians.

There were no vacant tables at the Cloiserie but Duthrey, who was evidently a habitué, recognized a friend dining alone and the two of them joined the man. Duthrey introduced him as François Vernot and Gautier remembered the name. Vernot was a young writer from a wealthy bourgeois family who had created a stir in Parisian literary circles a couple of years previously with an avant-garde novel. The book had attacked France and the French government so viciously that there had even been talk of a prosecution for sedition. People had also said that this modest success had so embittered Vernot that he was killing himself with ether and alcohol, but this evening he seemed cheerful enough.

'Don't tell me you two have been to see that preposterous melodrama, *La Dame*,' he said while Duthrey and Gautier were ordering their meal. 'Do you know that Dumas fils wrote the play in only eight days, to pay his debts?'

'We didn't go to see the play,' Duthrey explained. 'I wanted to see Monterant act.'

'That's the reason for the decline of the theatre today. People go to watch actors, not to see plays. A play has become just a vehicle for a well-known actor. And so the stage offers us nothing but the same old drawing-room comedies, the same old historical romances.'

'What about Ibsen, Strindberg and the rest of those gloomy

7

Scandinavians? We've had enough of them these last few years. And aren't you forgetting Antoine and Lugne-Poe?'

'One has to make an exception of Lugne-Poe,' Vernot admitted. 'He's the only theatrical producer of vision and intelligence in France today.'

'Does that mean,' Duthrey mocked him gently, 'that he's going to put on a play of yours?'

'As it happens he has promised to.'

'Well, I hope it gets a better reception than Jarry's.'

Duthrey was referring to the first performance of *Ubu Roi*, a play by Alfred Jarry which Lugne-Poe had staged a few years previously and which had been greeted by the audience with catcalls and cries of derision. It was *Ubu Roi* to which Duthrey had been alluding when he made disparaging remarks about modern drama to Gautier during the journey to the Cloiserie des Lilas. The play had earned the producer the unfortunate nickname of 'Lugne-Pot-de-chambre'.

'Make sure Gautier is invited to your première,' Duthrey told Vernot. 'He's a modernist too; prefers Monterant to the great Sarah.'

'My God, I should think so!'

'Of course I never saw Bernhardt when she was in her prime,' Gautier said. 'They tell me she was superb when she was with the Comédie-Française.'

'Her Phèdre was unmatchable,' Duthrey told him. 'The best ever.'

'Gautier and I are too young to know,' Vernot put in acidly. 'After all, the old harridan is not far short of sixty.'

'Sophie Monterant can live to be a hundred,' Duthrey said firmly, 'but she'll never die like Sarah does. No one has ever played a death scene as magnificently as Sarah. Think of how she died in *Fédora, Théodora, La Tosca*, not to mention *L'Aiglon*.'

The three of them continued to discuss the state of the theatre in France over their meal. Gautier found himself regretting that he could not contribute more to the conversation, but his knowledge of the contemporary stage was slender. As a young man he had sometimes been to the theatre with other students, joining them in the highest gallery as they shouted their approval or their

8

catcalls with traditional vigour. Later, as his career in the police began to take shape and after he had married, he seemed to have neither the time nor the inclination for the escape from reality which an evening at the Odéon or the Théâtre Porte-Saint-Martin afforded.

Had he found time, had he taken Suzanne out in the evenings sometimes to a theatre or even to a café-concert, they might still be together. The thought that his wife had left him for another man still disturbed him, not through vanity—he was not a vain man—but because it stirred a twinge of guilt. And ironically it was probably only because Suzanne had left him that he had been spending this evening at the Châtelet. Duthrey and his other friends, Gautier noticed, invited him out in the evenings from time to time and he suspected that they did it mainly through kindness, knowing that otherwise he would be alone.

When they had finished eating, two or three other diners joined them at their table to drink brandy. The conversation turned from the stage, almost inevitably, to politics. Not many years previously most people had believed France to have been on the brink of either a revolution or a military coup. Successive financial and political scandals, followed by the Dreyfus affair, had left the country bitter and neurotic, split into hostile factions: royalists and republicans, chauvinists and anarchists, militarists and paci-fists, anti-semites and intellectual pro-Jews. The Great Exposition of 1899 and the arrival of the new century had restored a large measure of stability and confidence, but the habit of political debate still lingered.

Once again Gautier contributed little to the discussion, not because he did not have political opinions but because he was con-scious that a policeman was supposed to be neutral. He was conscious too, that by talking freely in front of a policeman, his friends were showing their trust in him. It was not so many years ago that the government used to send spies, agents-provocateurs and even policemen into cafés to identify anarchists and other potential trouble-makers. Some people believed it still did.

The argument spun on, partisan but not acrimonious, until after midnight. They were the only customers left in the café when a messenger arrived from the offices of *Figaro*. Duthrey read the note which the man gave him, read it again, then got up from the table and drew Gautier to one side.

'Sophie Monterant is dead,' he said quietly.

Gautier stared at him incredulously. 'You can't be serious.'

'It's true, I am afraid. My people have just heard the news.'

'My God! Has she had an accident?'

'They appear to believe she was poisoned.'

2

SOPHIE MONTERANT'S apartment was on the third floor of a large house in Rue Murillo. The Plaine Monceau, as the district was called, had over the last few years become a fashionable place to live as wealthy bourgeois families followed the lead of some of the aristocracy and moved into the imposing houses in the vicinity of Parc Monceau.

The concierge, ill-tempered and sleepy, refused at first to admit Gautier and Duthrey to the building. A few years previously a wave of bombings by anarchists had produced panic bordering on hysteria among the concierges of Paris. Most of them had refused to admit a stranger after dark, fearful that he might be about to place a bomb in the building. Some had even refused to open the wicket door unless their tenants could identify themselves by saying a prearranged password. An unfortunate resident who forgot the password of the day might find himself left out in the streets all night.

When Gautier explained who he was, the woman did let them in, but grumbled that she had already admitted two policemen that evening, not to mention a doctor. As they climbed the stairs to Sophie Monterant's apartment, Duthrey remarked: 'It makes me feel almost guilty when I remember that less than an hour ago we were debating the ability of Monterant to play a death scene.'

In the apartment they found two policemen; a man from the commissariat of the eighth arrondissement and Inspector Lemaire, one of Gautier's colleagues from the Sûreté. The inspector was talking to the personal physician of the dead actress, a Dr Laradon.

Gautier explained to Lemaire that he had not come in any

official capacity, but that he had been dining with Duthrey when they had heard the news of the actress's death. He added: 'Duthrey may be able to help you as he has been collecting material for an article on the dead woman. I'll go and leave Duthrey with you, if you wish.'

'No need for that,' Lemaire replied. 'I'll be glad of your help.'

'How did she die?'

'Poison, so the doctor says.'

Hearing his name mentioned, Dr Laradon turned round. 'It would seem that Madame Monterant ate a chocolate containing cyanide,' he said.

'That can scarcely have been an accident.'

'No.' Lemaire pointed to a box containing chocolates which stood on the table behind him. 'Those are the chocolates.'

He explained to Gautier and Duthrey that the chocolates had been delivered to the apartment that afternoon. When Sophie Monterant had returned from the theatre, her maid had handed the box to her. She had eaten one of the chocolates and died almost at once.

'Where's the maid now?' Gautier asked.

'In her mistress's bedroom next door with the corpse.'

'The woman's in a bad state,' Dr Laradon said, 'Shock and grief. She seems to blame herself and refuses to leave her mistress. I've arranged for the body to be collected and taken to the mortuary and the sooner it's moved the better, in the interests of the maid.'

Gautier glanced round the room. Its décor, flamboyant but without style, showed that it had been lived in by an extrovert of constantly changing moods and whims. In the fashion of the day it was overcrowded not only with furniture, but with paintings, photographs, ornaments, bric-à-brac and personal mementos. In the centre was placed a chaise-longue draped with oriental silks on which, one supposed, the mistress of the house reclined to receive the homage of her admirers. On one wall hung a superb Chinese screen, but it was flanked by theatrical posters announcing performances of the Comédie Française, at the Gaiety Theatre in London and the Imperial Theatre in St Petersburg. Directly opposite these there was a portrait of Sophie Monterant in the chic, fashion-plate style which was becoming popular in France and this was surrounded by banal picture postcards interspersed with photographs of the actress in famous stage rôles: Phèdre, Jeanne d'Arc, Cléopâtre and inevitably the Dame aux Camélias. On the mantelpiece, the book-shelves and the cabinets were more theatrical mementos, a medallion struck to honour the return of Victor Hugo from exile after the fall of the Second Empire, a miniature plaster bust of Molière, a fan which had once belonged to Rachel and the quill pen with which de Musset was supposed to have written *Lorenzaccio*. They had been distributed, seemingly at random, among paperweights, coins, eighteenth-century miniatures and Venetian glass bowls, some valuable, others trivial and worthless.

Duthrey was questioning the doctor about the poisoned chocolates and Lemaire, who had clearly been waiting for such an opportunity, took Gautier on one side.

'Jean-Paul,' he said anxiously, 'I suppose you would not be willing to do me a tremendous service.'

Gautier smiled. 'That depends on what the service is.'

'I scarcely like to ask. Would you consider taking over the investigation into Monterant's death?'

'But I'm not on duty tonight.'

'I know, and I am. But as you may have heard my wife is expecting a child and although it's nowhere near her time, she's frightened at being left alone. There was a dreadful scene when I left her to come on duty this evening, I can tell you. In the normal way I might have been home by now, but this business could keep me occupied for hours.'

'So you want me to take over?'

'Is it asking too much?' Lemaire's eyes pleaded. 'After all, in a way you're already involved.'

What Lemaire really meant, Gautier knew, was that Gautier had no family obligations, no pregnant wife waiting hysterically at home, no wife at all to all intents and purposes.

'The director won't like it,' he said. 'You know what an obsession Courtrand has for regulations and discipline.'

'Oh, I can manage him. I can always tell him that I had an urgent message to go home as my wife thought her labour was beginning.'

13

Gautier shrugged and nodded his assent. He never minded working late nor doing more than his share of duties. Lemaire was right. There was no one at home waiting for him. And if it was not true that he was already involved in the death of Sophie Monterant, the circumstances of her death had certainly aroused in him that sharp curiosity which he knew he must experience if he were to investigate a crime effectively.

'Jean-Paul, you're a real friend!' Lemaire exclaimed, relieved and delighted. 'This is a debt I won't forget!'

He shook Gautier by the hand and hurried away to return to his nervous wife. Almost as he was leaving, two ambulance men arrived. Accompanied by the doctor, they took their stretcher into the adjoining bedroom and returned soon afterwards carrying the body of Sophie Monterant. Gautier was glad that it was covered with a blanket. He had never been squeamish, but he had no wish to see the features which had been animated with beauty only a few hours ago, frozen in a grimace of painful death. Behind the stretcher came a squat, dark woman in a black dress whom he took to be the maid and whose eyes were red with much weeping.

The ambulance men left, to carry their burden down three flights of narrow stairs. Doctor Laradon went with them and so did Duthrey, explaining that he must get back to the offices of *Figaro* to write his story. Gautier sent the policeman from the eighth arrondissement down with a message to the concierge, instructing her not to admit anyone to the building without first getting his authority.

Then he turned towards the maid. 'I have to ask you a few questions, Madame,' he told her.

'Mademoiselle,' she replied. 'Mademoiselle Françoise Bonnot.'

'Sit down, please.' Gautier pointed to a chair.

'No, Monsieur. That would not be right.'

'As you please. How long have you been working for your mistress?'

'Eight years, Monsieur. Ever since she left her parents' home to live on her own.'

'Do you live here?'

'Yes. I have a room on the fifth floor where all the servants of the building sleep.'

'And are you your mistress's only servant?'

'Yes. I do everything for her. We had a cook about a year ago who came in daily.' The memory of the cook appeared to fill Françoise with contempt. 'She only lasted a month. Everyone said my cooking was far better than that creature's!'

Gautier was beginning to recognize the woman as one of the rare, dwindling breed of servants, fanatically loyal and proud of their loyalty, jealous of her mistress's reputation, conservative, stubborn, and suspicious. Her thick, provençal accent suggested that Françoise came from the South.

'Tell me, Françoise,' Gautier pointed towards the box of chocolates on the table behind him. 'Where did these come from?'

'A messenger left them with the concierge.'

'At what time?'

'You'll have to ask her.' The concierge was obviously another enemy. 'I went out at about eight o'clock this evening to get some coffee, for we were running short and on my way back the concierge handed me the package.'

'And you gave it to your mistress when she returned from the theatre?'

'Yes.'

'I assume the box of chocolates was wrapped up in a parcel.'

For some reason Gautier's remark provoked more tears from Françoise. She blinked, forcing two large tears from her eyes which began to thread their way slowly down her heavily-lined face. 'It is all my fault that the poor lamb is dead. If only I had opened the parcel!'

'What difference would that have made?'

'I would have seen that they were chocolates.'

'So?'

'Madame hadn't eaten anything sweet for almost a month. She was worried about her figure, though as the good Lord knows, she had no cause to be. "Françoise," she told me, "if anyone sends me bon-bons or chocolates or cakes, keep them away from me. I don't wish to be tempted." So I would usually open the parcels and do as she had said.'

'Then how was it that she ate one of the chocolates this time?'

'She said she would have just one to celebrate her success in the

15

new play. "I have resisted temptation tonight," she told me, "for he wished to take me to supper after the theatre and I refused. So surely I can allow myself the indulgence of one chocolate?" You see, she wanted to go to bed early tonight and be ready for to-morrow. Madame always said that the second performance of a play was even more important than the first. The first was for the critics, but the second for the theatre-goers, the people.'

Wiping the tears away with her sleeve, she sobbed aloud, small plaintive cries like those of a frightened child.

'Who was this man who asked her to supper?' Gautier asked.

Françoise stopped sobbing and stared at him resentfully. He realized that she was lying as she replied: 'I do not know, Mon-sieur.'

'Was there a card with the box?'

'Yes, it's lying on the table there. But all it says is that the choco-lates are from an admirer. She had a lot of gifts like that.'

Gautier looked at the chocolates again. They were in a circular box, covered in apple-green velvet and with a lid decorated with sprigs of artificial lily-of-the-valley. Only one chocolate was miss-ing from the top of two layers.

'Where are the paper and string with which the box was wrapped?'

'I took them to the kitchen.'

'I'll take them with me as well as the box when I leave. But first I have to seal the apartment. You must go to your room, Françoise, and neither you nor anyone else is to be allowed into this apartment until I return tomorrow morning. I'll instruct the concierge accordingly as I leave.'

Françoise looked at him suspiciously. 'Why are you coming back?'

'To make a thorough search of the apartment and of all your mistress's belongings.'

'I won't allow it!' the maid said with a sudden spurt of anger. 'You have no right to start prying into her life!'

'We have every right,' Gautier replied firmly. 'As part of our investigations into an unlawful killing.'

'You flics! Have you no respect for anything or anyone? Not even for the dead?'

'Be sensible, Françoise. Don't you want us to find out who sent these poisoned chocolates to your mistress?'

Françoise stared at him. Her expression was as hard and unemotional as her voice when she replied: 'Monsieur, I already know who sent them.'

3

EARLY NEXT MORNING in his office at the headquarters of the Sûreté on Quai des Orfèvres, Gautier wrote a preliminary report on the death of Sophie Monterant. He had arrived at the Sûreté earlier than he was obliged to, partly because he wished to write the report in peace and undisturbed, but also because he enjoyed walking through Paris while the city was just awakening.

From his home on the Left Bank he had sauntered through streets that were silent and empty except for an occasional cart taking farm produce from the country to the market at Les Halles. Here and there a café was just opening its doors, the owner getting ready for the early morning trade of men who liked to take their breakfast—and very often a marc as well—on their way to work.

Crossing to the Ile de la Cité by the Pont St Michel, Gautier had stopped for a time by the Seine. The bright May sunlight made even the tired, grey waters seem fresh and alive. His office in the Sûreté headquarters overlooked the Seine and he never tired of watching the river. Some people, he knew, thought of it as a boundary, dividing two very different halves of Paris: art, fashion and wealth on one side, politics, learning and unrest on the other. For Gautier it was more than a boundary, it was the face of Paris, reflecting her changing moods, sullen and angry or thoughtful and introspective or careless and happy.

Now, seated at his desk, he resisted the temptation to look at the river again and wrote his report. It was brief and factual, no more than an account of the circumstances of Sophie Monterant's death and of Dr Laradon's opinion as to its cause. He made no mention of his conversation with Françoise, nor of her claim that she knew the identity of the person who had sent her mistress the poisoned chocolates.

The maid had surprised him by naming as the murderer a

celebrity, Clémentine Lyse, who was one of the best-known singers in the café-concerts of Paris. According to Françoise, this was the last act in a bitter feud between the actress and the singer which had started years previously when the two of them had been pupils together at the Conservatoire, a feud based on Clémentine Lyse's jealous hatred of Monterant. The suggestion, unsupported by any evidence, seemed more than improbable to Gautier. He could see no reason why the singer, who was one of the most popular performers in the caf'conc's, who would be better known to most Parisians and almost certainly earned more money than Monterant, should wish to kill the actress through jealousy. So he decided to make no mention of Françoise's allegations in his report, which would become part of the permanent records of the case.

When he had finished writing, he took the report down to the office of the Director of the Sûreté, which was on the first floor of the building, and placed it on Courtrand's desk. The building was beginning to stir with activity as the staff, clerks as well as police officers, arrived for duty. When he returned to his own room, he found Surat, who was his principal assistant, waiting for him.

Surat was a man in late middle-age, approaching retirement, and a policeman of the old school. Conscientious, trustworthy and brave, he had been somehow passed by for promotion, although his loyalty and efficiency could not be doubted. Gautier sometimes wondered cynically what were the qualities needed to win recognition and success in the Sûreté and he had even analysed his own character to decide whether he could identify any of them there.

Now he first told Surat the facts about Sophie Monterant's death and then showed him the box of chocolates which he had brought back from Rue Murillo the previous night. He held the box up and pointed at a small, printed label on the bottom.

'We can see that the chocolates came from Labiche in Rue de la Paix,' he said. 'But before we try to find out who might have bought them, I wish to have them examined.'

'You want me to take them to the government laboratories?'

'Yes. Ask them to analyse the remaining chocolates to see whether any more of them contain poison. It is not likely that if anyone planned to kill La Monterant, they would put only one

19

poisoned chocolate in the box and rely on her eating it. If it turns out that any of the remaining chocolates have also been poisoned I would like to know how it was done.'

As Surat began to wrap the box up in its brown paper, Gautier continued: 'Ask the chemists if they can let you have the results as soon as they can. Today if possible.'

'You're an optimist. Scientists like to take their time and people in government service even more so.'

'You're probably right. Anyway, in the meantime you can be carrying out another small task. I would like a few facts about the caf'conc' singer, Clémentine Lyse. Just routine information: where she was born, where she lives, whether she is married and if not whether she lives alone.'

'Facts, not hearsay?'

'Precisely. We may have to widen the scope of our enquiries later, but not yet. And, oh yes, find out at what caf'conc' she is singing now and the times of her performances each day.'

'Does that mean you're going to see her on the stage?'

'Yes. I wish to form my own impression of the lady and not to rely on gossip and servant talk.'

'Anything else, Patron?'

'There will be more later, no doubt, but that should be enough for the present.'

Having put Surat to work, Gautier decided he could leave the office with a clear conscience. Administration, the writing of reports, checking of statements and allotting duties to junior officers did not suit his restless nature and he was always glad of an excuse to get away from headquarters. Leaving the Sûreté, he crossed the river to Rue de Rivoli and took an omnibus heading north-west.

The drivers of Paris omnibuses were always unpredictable and the one in charge of the vehicle he took was in a leisurely mood. He allowed the horses to amble gently along Rue de Rivoli before turning past the Palais Royal into Avenue de l'Opéra. Having climbed precariously up the narrow stairs to the 'impériale' or upper deck, Gautier could sit enjoying the sunshine and the scene below. The streets were beginning to fill up, mainly with fiacres and carriages. Motor cars were still relatively few in Paris and as their owners were to be found almost exclusively in the leisured classes, they were not usually to be seen in the streets until later in the day, taking wealthy bankers to their offices, gentlemen to the Bois de Boulogne for their morning equestrian exercise or ladies to call on each other as part of the social round.

Leaving the omnibus at the corner of Boulevard Haussmann and Boulevard Malesherbes, he walked up to Rue Murillo. The concierge was sitting in her room inside the gate knitting, while a fat baby, presumably one of her grandchildren, was crawling round her feet. Gautier reminded her that he was from the Sûreté and that it was he whom she had admitted to the house the previous evening.

'Is it true that Madame Monterant was poisoned?' she asked him curiously. 'I saw them taking her away last night.'

'Yes, it's true.'

'Then what's to be done about the apartment?'

'No doubt you'll be told in due course by Madame Monterant's relatives or her lawyers. For the present you can help me by answering one question.'

'What's that?'

'A parcel was delivered here yesterday for the dead woman. I want to know at what time you received it.'

'I gave it to the maid, Françoise, in the evening.'

'That isn't what I asked you.'

The concierge got up and retrieved the baby, which had crawled away from her feet and was heading for a coal-bucket. She replied to Gautier's question over her shoulder.

'How should I know what time the parcel came? I don't wear a watch.'

'You must have some idea. Was it long before Françoise collected it? One hour? Two hours?'

'Of course it wasn't long,' the woman said sullenly, 'otherwise I'd have taken it upstairs to the apartment. That's my job.'

'And who delivered it?'

'I don't know.'

'Was it a boy or girl?'

'A boy, I think. But how do you expect me to remember? People come in and out of this building all day. I don't have time to look at them all. They pay me to be a concierge, not a sentry.'

21

The baby was crawling away again, so she grabbed it and smacked it angrily on the leg. Frustrated and indignant, the baby retaliated by beginning to scream. Recognizing defeat, Gautier left and climbed the stairs to the third floor. The policeman from the eighth arrondissement whom he had left on duty the previous night had been replaced by another. Gautier asked him whether he had seen the maid that morning.

'Oh, yes, Monsieur l'Inspecteur!' the man laughed. 'She's been hanging around keeping an eye on me. She doesn't trust the police, that one.'

'Well, find her and bring her to me, will you please? And I want you here as witness as well, when I remove the seals from the door to the apartment.'

Françoise could not have been far away, for the policeman returned with her in not much more than a minute. Gautier had sealed the apartment the previous night by the simple expedient of placing strips of tape right across the double front doors and affixing them to the wall on each side with blobs of sealing-wax into which he had pressed the official police stamp. He showed the policeman and Françoise that the seals were intact and then broke them to release the tapes.

Inside the drawing-room was still in darkness, the air heavy and stale. It could only have been his imagination but Gautier thought he could detect a smell of cyanide. While Françoise was drawing the curtains apart, he made a quick tour of the apartment. Besides the drawing-room he found a dining-room, a large bedroom, a smaller room which served as a boudoir and a kitchen. All of them except the kitchen were furnished with the almost eccentric lack of style so noticeable in the drawing-room. The kitchen, on the other hand, was a countrywoman's kitchen, methodically clean but redolent of pungent country smells: onions and peppers, garlic and black olives.

He found the writing bureau he was looking for in the bedroom. In his experience the clues to a woman's life were usually to be found in a writing desk. Sophie Monterant's desk was locked so he turned to Françoise, who had been following him from room to room suspiciously, as she might watch a plumber whom she did not trust at work.

'Where did your mistress keep the key to this bureau?' he asked her.

'I don't know.'

'You might just as well tell me,' he said, not unkindly although she was obviously lying, 'because otherwise it will be damaged when I force it open.'

Françoise stared at him rebelliously for a moment. Then she crossed to the dressing-table, took a jewel box from one of the drawers and from the jewel box a key which she handed to him.

Gautier was surprised to find that the bureau was meticulously tidy. Actresses, he had always supposed, would be casual and care-less, like artists too engrossed in ideas and in their art to worry overmuch about method and system and the other disciplines needed for an orderly life. Sophie Monterant, however, had arranged her papers, letters and other documents neatly and had kept them separated in the pigeon-holes and drawers of the bureau.

He found two bundles of bills, the larger all paid and receipted, while the others were waiting to be paid. Several of the bills, he noticed, had been checked and corrected where there had been errors in addition. The mistakes were usually quite small, amounting to only a franc or two. Business correspondence with theatrical producers, costumiers, managers and playwrights was arranged separately, the letters clipped together according to the theatre or production to which they related.

In the pigeon-holes of the desk were three books: two bound in dark-blue leather and the other a cheap accounts book with two columns for figures. One of the leather-bound books contained addresses and the other was an engagement book. In the accounts book household purchases had been entered in clumsy, laborious handwriting which Gautier suspected must be that of Françoise and here again the figures had been carefully checked and corrected where necessary.

The desk, Gautier realized, was that of a business woman and contained nothing personal, no private letters, no photographs or mementos, nothing that could be remotely connected with the owner's private life. Disappointed, he decided even so that the engagement and address books might both conceivably contain

23

information related to his investigation and that he would be justified in taking them with him back to the Sûreté.

As he was shutting the bureau, he glanced up into an oval mirror framed in seashells which hung on the wall above it. In it he could see that Francoise, who had been standing behind him, had moved quietly away to a table by the bed on the opposite side of the room. As he watched she opened a drawer in the table, took something out and hid it beneath her apron.

He waited until she came towards him and then said: 'All right, Françoise, you can give that to me.'

'What, Monsieur?'

'Whatever you just took from the drawer of the bedside table.'

'I took nothing,' she replied stubbornly.

Gautier was beginning to lose patience, much as he admired loyalty. He told the maid roughly: 'Either you hand it to me now or you'll be arrested, taken to the local police commissariat and searched.'

The threat succeeded in breaking down Françoise's defiance. For an honest countrywoman the humiliation of being taken away by the police was too much to face. Sullenly she brought out what she had been concealing and handed it to Gautier. It was yet another blue leather book, this time a diary.

'And why were you trying to hide this from me?' Gautier asked her. 'What secrets did your mistress have that you don't wish me to learn?'

'I don't know what you mean.'

'Is it the names of her lovers, perhaps?' Gautier was only guessing but sometimes one learned much from the replies to wild guesses. 'Was one of them causing trouble? Or was it a jealous wife?'

The remark did not provoke the reaction he had expected. Françoise merely looked at him with something like contempt as she replied: 'Men? How could any man have caused her trouble? She did what she wanted with them. Actors, politicians, generals, aristocrats, she treated them all like fools, which is what they were.'

When he arrived back at Sûreté headquarters, Gautier found a message waiting for him to say that the director wished to see the

24

inspector as a matter of extreme urgency. Messages phrased in that way usually meant that Courtrand was displeased and today's was no exception.

Gautier found him in his office, pacing up and down as he admonished his secretary for some petty breach of clerical routine. Courtrand was a traditionalist, almost fanatical in his reverence for protocol and regulations, as well as for convention. The frock coat which he always wore by day and his small, neat beard would have lent him the dignity and authority he sought, if only he could always have remained seated. Sadly, however, he was a short man and not even the corsets he was known to wear could conceal his paunchiness, so that standing, and even more so pacing up and down, he looked ridiculous, an arrogant, ill-tempered bantam cock.

'What's this I hear, Gautier?' he demanded, when he had finished rebuking his secretary. 'Is it true you've taken over an investigation that Lemaire should be handling?'

'He has problems at home, Monsieur le Directeur.'

'Oh, yes, I know all about his wretched wife. Who doesn't? But that must not be allowed to interfere with his work. Hasn't the woman got a mother to be with her on these occasions?'

'Her mother is dead, I understand.'

'Then what about Lemaire's mother?'

'His parents live in Lille.'

Gautier knew that Courtrand, in spite of his pompousness, was a kind man at heart who looked after the welfare of his staff. He did not believe that Lemaire's domestic problems could be the real cause of the director's anger, which he recognized from experience as a symptom of anxiety. Some more serious matter must be worrying Courtrand and he waited to be told of it.

'This is most inconvenient!' Courtrand complained. 'I require your assistance, Gautier, on another matter.'

'What's that, Monsieur?'

'Pelotti has been arrested. They picked him up on the Italian border, travelling by the night train to Milan.'

'That's good news! The Prefect of Police will be delighted.'

'It was a stroke of luck, I can tell you. The scoundrel was travelling first class, if you please, in a wagon-lit, with a false passport

25

and plenty of money. He might easily have been mistaken for a gentleman!'

Marcel Pelotti was a criminal who had plagued the Paris police for a dozen years or more. Of Italian extraction, he had started as a young man in petty crime, living on the immoral earnings of women and a little extortion. Then suddenly one day he had emerged as a self-professed anarchist, speaking at public meetings with Louise Michel and writing—or signing—articles for *L'Intransigeant*. He had been arrested, indicted and tried three times on charges of planting bombs in the apartments of judges and politicians but in every case had been acquitted for lack of evidence.

In recent years less had been heard of his politics and more of his sex life. As anarchism became unfashionable, he had turned his attention to women. Strikingly handsome, Pelotti also had style and panache enough to make even quite respectable women forget his criminal background. It was rumoured that ladies from the 'gratin' or upper crust of society were among those who were prepared to reward his favours with money or expensive gifts.

Until a couple of weeks back, life had appeared to have been treating Pelotti more than kindly. He had dressed well, ate well, lived well, without, as far as the Paris police who kept a continuous watch on him could tell, breaking the law.

Then one morning Lucie Bertron was found dead in her apartment. Lucie was a well-known cocotte, not quite in the class of Liane de Pougy or Caroline Otéro, the two leading courtesans or 'horizontals' of Paris, but even so she was attractive enough to have excited the interest of the then Prince of Wales and expensive enough to have a carriage of her own, upholstered in yellow satin and pulled by four splendid black horses.

Marks on Lucie's body had shown that she had been badly beaten before her neck had been broken. She was known to have been friendly with Marcel Pelotti, in fact their relationship had been the subject of slanderous comment in the press. He had been seen riding in her carriage through the Bois de Boulogne, dining with her at Maxim's, escorting her to the theatre. Lucie's maid had testified that he often spent the night at her apartment and, more important, that he had been there on the night of her death. A baker delivering bread the following morning had seen a man resembling Pelotti leaving the apartment carrying a suitcase. As if to confirm his guilt, Pelotti had then disappeared, going to ground like the criminal he was, in the underworld of Paris.

'Would you like me to hand over the Monterant investigation to someone else?' Gautier asked Courtrand.

'Not now you have started work on the case. No, I will have to handle the Pelotti affair myself.' Courtrand looked at Gautier thoughtfully for a moment as though he were trying to decide how the inspector could be fitted into a plan he was devising. 'But you'll have to assist me.'

'In what way, Monsieur le Directeur?'

'It's just a small thing. Pelotti is being brought back by train under escort. He arrives at the Gare de Lyon at four-thirty this afternoon. I want you to go and collect him and bring him back here.'

'I can easily do that,' Gautier replied, wondering at the same time why he was being asked to do this errand. Collecting a prisoner from a station was clearly not a job for the Director of the Sûreté, but there were plenty of policemen available to do it.

Courtrand must have realized what he would be thinking, because he said: 'This business may not be as straightforward as it appears. That's why I want you rather than any other inspector to collect Pelotti from the station and that's why I intend to question him myself. Take two officers with you to the station but on the way back you must ride alone with him in the waggon. No one apart from yourself is to see Pelotti before I do.'

Instead of satisfying Gautier's curiosity, Courtrand's instructions only sharpened it. In the normal way, Courtrand only took a personal interest in Sûreté investigations which might have political repercussions or those which were in any way connected with important people. His appointment as head of the Sûreté had been a case of political patronage, a reward for past services to the government of the day and he would spare no effort to see that his patrons were not embarrassed by any scandal.

Pelotti was a criminal who was being arrested on the suspicion that he might have killed a woman who, although well-known in the demi-monde, was of no consequence in either the social or political scene. Gautier could see nothing in the business to justify Courtrand's interest or the elaborate precautions he was taking in Pelotti's arrest. Courtrand was not, however, a man who liked to have his motives questioned.

'Are there any other special instructions, Monsieur?' he asked.

'No,' Courtrand replied. 'Except that you must be discreet. Remember, Gautier, I am relying on your discretion.'

4

BACK IN HIS own office, Gautier examined the three leather-bound books which he had brought back from Sophie Monterant's apartment. In the address book he found the private addresses of several distinguished people including an aged duke who was then the President of the Jockey Club; Nathaniel Granz, said to be the third richest banker in France; the Minister of Beaux-arts, Henri Charvet; the current German ambassador in Paris, and General Jacques Lafitte. The name of Clémentine Lyse, the singer whom Françoise had accused of killing her mistress, was not listed.

The engagement book did not appear to have much to offer that might have any bearing on Sophie Monterant's death. She had used it only for business engagements, meetings with producers or playwrights, interviews with journalists or with her accountant, appointments with costumiers. Later it might be useful as a means of checking on the dead woman's movements over the previous few days, but for the time being Gautier put it on one side.

The diary looked more promising, for it had been conscientiously kept, with an entry recorded for practically every day. Knowing that it had been kept by the actress's bedside, Gautier had assumed that she had written in it at night before retiring. Thus he was not surprised to find no entry for the day on which she had been killed. Turning to the previous day he read:

Monday, May 14th
The final rehearsal for La Dame passed off well enough. Creuze irritates some of the cast by his too meticulous direction, but at least he has the sense to leave me complete freedom of expression. The costumiers have made a complete travesty of my dress for the final scene—it hangs on me like a man's night-shirt. Their

29

excuse of course is that I have lost so much weight in the last month which is scarcely true. Rimrod looked in at the theatre towards the end and came back for supper afterwards. He was very amorous and I was forced to restrain his passion, explaining that I had to save my energy for tomorrow. He sulked a little but I promised to make it up to him on Sunday. Had a petit bleu from Spumantisi in the afternoon, wishing me luck for tomorrow. I hope he keeps his promise to attend. It would lend quite a cachet to the first performance.

Glancing back through the entries for the previous month, Gautier found several references to the man named as Rimrod, which made it clear that their friendship had been much more than platonic. A cynic might also have wondered whether the actress had counted on more from her lover than just affection. An entry dated near the end of April read:

Rimrod and I had supper at Webers and he gave me an exquisite pair of diamond ear-rings, which he had made for me by Cartier to his own design. They must have cost at least a hundred thousand francs. After supper he came back to Rue Murillo and how could I refuse him?

Nor had Rimrod's generosity been confined to giving the actress expensive presents. Gautier learned that he had, it appeared, been one of those who had provided the finance to stage *La Dame Aux Camélias* at the Châtelet. A week before the play had been due to open, the diary reported:

Rimrod's wife has learned that he is one of my backers for La Dame, but according to him she doesn't mind at all. Evidently she told him mockingly that she was delighted to know of his sudden interest in culture, for she had been coming to believe that the only thing he understood or cared about was horses. I find her attitude hard to understand. If it was my husband, I'd kill him. After all, it is her money.

As he read back through the entries, Gautier found that while

30

most of the people mentioned were referred to by their real names, in a number of cases Sophie Monterant had preferred to use what appeared to be code names of her own invention. In addition to 'Rimrod' and 'Spumantisi', he found 'Labiste' and 'Jockey' and 'Monge'. It was only for men that she had used this device and even then not for all men. Many actors, producers and writers were named quite openly and the obvious conclusion was that the code names were only used to conceal the identities of a few intimate men friends.

For no very logical reason, he had already begun to believe that the reason why Sophie Monterant had been poisoned would be connected with a relationship with a man. This did not mean that he had already written it down as a 'crime passionel'; on the contrary, the impression he was forming of the dead woman, from her manner and her acting on the stage, from the décor of her apartment and from what he had read in her diary, was that love and passion had played little part in her life.

Even so, she had not lacked the ability to rouse passion in others. An entry in the diary dated about a month previously read:

Monge arrived uninvited before lunch in a storm of jealousy. He has found out that after I sent him away last Thursday, pleading a headache, Rimrod came to the apartment for supper. I told him that Rimrod's wife has great influence in the theatrical world but his only comment was: 'In that case why aren't you receiving the wife late at night, instead of the husband?' Finally I grew bored with his tantrums and told him I would have as many men friends as I chose and added that Rimrod was younger, more amusing and more virile than him. He grew so angry that I thought he was going to hit me, but, like most soldiers, brave though he might be on the battlefield, he's a moral coward. He left in a sulk. I wonder how he did find out about Rimrod's visit. Is it Françoise trying to run my life as usual? She dislikes Rimrod for some reason.

As he read it, Gautier realized that by itself the diary was not likely to tell him much. Before he could understand the significance of what Sophie Monterant had written and the events she had described, he must be able to identify the men with whom she had been on intimate terms and whom she had given the made-up names. Any one of them—or their wives—might have had a motive for wishing the actress dead, but speculation would be pointless until he knew who they were.

The maid Françoise could probably guess their identities, but he did not believe for one moment that she would tell him. The gossips of Paris or any woman of the theatre would certainly be able to give him a clue, but, as he did not know any, he would have to try the next best source: the newspapers.

It was past midday so he locked the diary and the other books away, left the Sûreté and strolled in the sunshine to the Café Corneille on Boulevard St Germain. The hour of the apéritif had arrived and the habitués of the café would be gathering there: lawyers, politicians, a businessman or two and, among the most faithful of the clientèle, Duthrey of *Figaro*.

When he reached the Corneille, Duthrey had not arrived, but other friends and acquaintances were there to welcome him to join them and sip a glass of port. The conversation today was not about the law nor politics nor the arts, but about a scandal which had shaken Paris earlier that week. Passionate and compromising letters between a young German aristocrat, Baron Friedrich Van Golingen and a French boy of good family had been intercepted by the boy's father. The baron, who had been attached to the German embassy in Paris, had been hastily recalled to Berlin, but not before the scandal broke and instead of leaving for home he had shot himself.

No mention was made of Sophie Monterant, which could only mean that the story had not yet appeared in the newspapers. Gautier was relieved because, although his friends at the Café Corneille respected his official position and never tried to discuss police matters with him, their self-imposed restraint always made him feel slightly ill at ease. Sometimes he thought of himself as being excluded from their circle, an outsider, like a priest in front of whom men stopped swearing, talking of sex and telling scabrous stories.

'Why should a man kill himself because he's a pédé?' a young lawyer sitting opposite Gautier was saying. 'Because he's an aristocrat? There are plenty of homosexuals in all walks of life: actors, journalists, poets by the score, even lawyers.'

'Among the aristocracy too, if it comes to that,' another lawyer remarked. 'What about Prince Constantin Radziwill? He has twelve handsome footmen to each of whom he has given a present of a superb pearl necklace.'

'The baron was a diplomat,' said an elderly deputy from Seine-et-Marne. 'His career was destroyed.'

'But why should it be?'

'Men in public service must live to higher standards. They must be above not only reproach but above suspicion.'

'We have plenty in the public services of France whose private lives would not bear close examination.'

'No doubt,' the deputy agreed, 'but they are selective in their vices. Women, gambling, a little peculation on the side, these a Frenchman can understand, forgive and even admire. But homosexuality? Never!'

Gautier pulled out his pocket watch. A handsome hunter, it had been a present to him from Suzanne's father on their fifth wedding anniversary. The case had an unsightly dent, the mark of a knife with which some cut-throat had tried to stab Gautier late one night when he was walking home from Montmartre. His father-in-law's gift, if it had not actually saved his life, had protected him from serious injury when, ironically, he had been returning from an evening spent with Claudine, his mistress at that time. Although the incident had taken place after Suzanne had already left him, Gautier thought of the watch as a symbol, a reminder that he shared the blame for the failure of their marriage.

The watch told him it was approaching one o'clock and he realized that Duthrey would not be coming to the Corneille that day. The journalist was a man of regular and precise habits and no professional commitment nor social distraction ever prevented him from arriving home at exactly one o'clock for his lunch. Gautier decided that he would go and find something to eat himself, but as he was finishing his glass of port another journalist, Cros from *Le Matin*, arrived.

Cros belonged to an entirely different breed of journalists from Duthrey and one which Gautier disliked and distrusted. Acquisitive, cunning and without scruples, when it came to getting a story, Cros had no regard for integrity or privacy and very little for truth. Success in his career had made him boastful and arrogant.

'Well, gentlemen,' he said, pulling up a chair to join the group. 'Soon we'll have no beautiful women left in Paris, will we?'

'What do you mean?' the deputy asked.

'Another one was done to death last night.'

'Who?'

'The actress Sophie Monterant. She was the victim of a poisoner.' Cros looked towards Gautier and grinned. 'That's right, isn't it, Inspector?'

'We have to wait for an official report from the government laboratories before the cause of death can be announced,' Gautier replied.

Cros laughed. 'Fortunately we in the press are not tied by bureaucratic regulations. La Monterant died last evening after eating a poisoned chocolate from a box sent to her as a gift. You can read the whole story in the next edition of *Le Matin*.'

'Are you saying she was murdered?'

'It was no accident, I can tell you that. We even know who sent Monterant the chocolates.'

'What!' exclaimed the lawyer. 'Don't tell us you are going to name the man in your columns?'

'It wasn't a man, but a woman. No, we can hardly give the actual name but what we do say is that she is a famous caf'conc' singer.'

'What you really mean is that you have no proof,' Gautier said contemptuously. 'My God, Cros, you would publish anything if you thought it would sell your miserable newspaper!'

'Come now, Inspector,' Cros replied insolently, 'you must not take offence just because we move more quickly than you.' Turning to the others he laughed. 'It isn't only justice that is blindfolded, but the police as well.'

Gautier lunched off cassoulet, cheese and a half-bottle of red wine in a restaurant not far from Les Halles. The cassoulet was heavy and pungent, but no worse than one had the right to expect in a restaurant in that district. He had learned to live with second-rate

34

cuisine and lonely meals, but it did not improve his temper to know that his colleagues would be in their homes eating meals prepared with the skill and patience of bourgeois wives.

His ill-temper sprang not so much from his brush with Cros at the Café Corneille, but from a realization that the story *Le Matin* would be publishing could only have been based on a talk with Sophie Monterant's maid. Gautier knew now that he should have taken stronger action to prevent Françoise from speaking to journalists. His instinct told him that the libellous rumours which *Le Matin* was publishing would, far from throwing any light on the actress's death, only cause complications and trouble. He sometimes wished that the French press had, like English newspapers, to take some account of libel laws.

When he arrived back at the Sûreté, there was an envelope waiting for him which did a little to lighten his gloom. It was a note from Duthrey which said simply that Gautier might be interested to read the article which Duthrey had written about Sophie Monterant and which would be appearing in the next edition of *Figaro*. Attached to the note were seven sheets of paper covered in Duthrey's elegant, though rather formal handwriting. Although the typewriter was now coming slowly into general use, Duthrey had sworn that everything he would ever write for *Figaro* would be in his own hand. He was inordinately proud of his script and with good reason. The article read:

SOPHIE MONTERANT PLAYS HER LAST TRAGEDY
A brilliant career ended by poison
Our readers will have learned elsewhere in this issue of the tragic death of the actress Sophie Monterant.

Only a few hours before she died I was one of the many thousands of Parisians who were present in the Châtelet theatre at the first performance of a new production of *La Dame aux Camélias* in which Madame Monterant played the rôle of Marguerite. As we saw her emulate death with a pathos that moved us all to pity, how could we have known that soon she would in reality be dying?

The première was a triumph. Madame Monterant's performance is reviewed, also elsewhere in this issue, by our dramatic critic. What I intend to write about is the woman herself, her personality, her private life, the remorselessness with which she drove herself to her triumphs, her disastrous marriage and her tumultuous love affairs.

Sophie Monterant was born twenty-eight years ago in Paris. Her father, a lawyer who specialized in marine litigation, also had an office and a house in Le Havre and much of the girl's childhood was spent in the old seaport. When I spoke with her only a few days ago, she told me of the happy memories of her infancy, of being taken by her governess to see the great ships in the harbour, of her dreams that one day she too would travel across the oceans and visit exotic places.

After her schooling at the Convent of the Little Sisters, Sophie decided that she wished to become an actress and at the age of sixteen she took the entrance examination for the Conservatoire. As our readers will know, competition for entry to France's great academy of dramatic art is always intense, but the judges were quick to see the promise of the young Mlle Monterant and she was accepted as a pupil. Her period of study was a triumph of brilliance, as she won first prizes for both Tragedy and Comedy. The Minister of Beaux-arts at that time, Monsieur Pierre Druot, was so impressed with her ability that he used his influence to secure for her when she left the Conservatoire, the highest honour that an aspiring young actress can win, an engagement with the Comédie-Française.

She made her début shortly afterwards in Racine's *Iphigénie en Aulide* and my late colleague, the great dramatic critic, F. Sarcey, wrote thus of her first performance: 'Mlle Monterant has a fine posture, graceful movements and a good diction. How refreshing it is to find a young actress who is not afraid to *speak* her lines and not mumble obscurely in the Scandinavian manner. She should go far.'

In an amazingly short time Sophie Monterant had established herself in France's national theatre and was playing leading rôles. Indeed her success was so swift that it provoked the jealousy of others and soon it was being rumoured that she owed her success not to her ability but to the favours she was granting Camille Terin, the Director of the Comédie-Française.

Many people expected that she would stay with the Maison de Molière and become one of the great classical tragediennes of all time. It was not to be and soon her career was being beset by storms and sensations.

First, while playing in London she met the English actor, James Henry, a man fully twenty years older than herself and of a doubtful reputation, said to have been an intimate of Oscar Wilde. Their love affair was short but spectacular. Within hours of meeting, they left London together for Venice, Sophie abandoning her commitments with the Comédie-Française without a thought and without warning. After a passionate month in the city of canals, they came to Paris and began rehearsals for a production of *Macbeth* in which they were to perform together. The play, like their romance, was stillborn. Within a few days Henry left suddenly for London and soon afterwards the new Madame Henry began proceedings for divorce.

Ironically enough it was on the dungheap of her departure from the Comédie-Française and of her scandalous marriage that Sophie Monterant's career in the theatre grew and flourished. From that day on her every venture succeeded. Audiences flocked to see her perform, drawn perhaps by the notoriety that surrounded her name. Her greatest following was among young people, who admired the bravado with which she flouted convention. More than once students waited for her outside the theatre and then drew her carriage in a triumphant procession to some café on the Left Bank.

There were more scandals and more sensations. On one occasion she appeared on the stage naked in Wilde's *Salomé* and was threatened with police prosecution; then the wife of General Jacques Lafitte, with whom Sophie was rumoured to be having a love affair, went in a frenzy of jealousy to the actress's apartment armed with a revolver and tried to shoot her. On another occasion Prince Gregoire of Roumania declared that he would offer a diamond necklace worth 250,000 francs to spend a single night with her and soon afterwards Sophie appeared at a lunch in honour of Lucien Guitry wearing a splendid diamond necklace that no one had seen her wear before.

And what of the woman herself? Disparaging adjectives have

often been used to describe Sophie Monterant; adjectives like cruel, ruthless and egotistical. In my long conversations with her, when she spoke of her likes and her dislikes, her dreams and her disappointments, I detected no cruelty in her. What I found was a truly dedicated artist, a woman for whom her chosen profession was all. As a perfectionist, she had only one goal—to be the greatest actress in France. To achieve that goal she was prepared to work unceasingly and, if necessary, to sacrifice what ordinary people value most—home, friendship, emotions, love. If she believed she had attained that goal, then I do not think she would have cared if the words 'ruthless' and 'egotistical' were to appear in her epitaph.

The article told Gautier less than he had hoped. Other journalists and other newspapers, even though publishing what was in effect an obituary of Sophie Monterant, would have had much more to say about her private life, naming her friends, her lovers and perhaps even her enemies. Gautier was not altogether surprised. A long acquaintance had taught him that by the current standards of French journalism, Duthrey was a writer of restraint and good taste.

Even so, the article had given him one name, a possible starting point and he decided to use it. Leaving his office he went down to see Corbin, the personal assistant to the Director-General of the Sûreté.

Corbin, who worked in a room not much larger than a broom cupboard next to Courtrand's imposing office, was a man who could be described accurately and vividly in three words—he was a French civil servant. He had all the qualities and the failings of the 'petit fonctionnaire'. Painstaking, patient and slow, he was proud of his métier and jealous of his responsibilities. He served his chief faithfully and, because Courtrand was much obsessed with important people, Corbin had slowly and determinedly amassed a detailed knowledge of the people in France who mattered, not actresses of course nor caf'conc' singers, but politicians, diplomats and the last remaining figures of the old French aristocracy as well as the emigré bankers and wealthy Americans who were sustaining these old families.

When Gautier went into his room, Corbin was staring out of the window. He might have been mentally composing a poem, for following the example of many other French civil servants like de Maupassant and Verlaine, he was a writer whose poems were published from time to time in literary reviews, delicate verses in obscure old metres like the Villanelle.

'What do you know about General Jacques Lafitte?' Gautier asked him.

'The former Minister of War?'

'Was he ever minister?' Gautier asked in surprise.

'You might be forgiven for not noticing the event,' Corbin said drily. 'His ministry lasted for only five months: one of the shortest in the history of France.'

'Why? Did he misbehave?'

'No, he was just incompetent.'

'What else can you tell me about the general?'

In a cupboard in his room, Corbin had arranged in alphabetical order on a shelf a row of folders, each tied with red tape. He went to the cupboard and took out one of the folders, from which he extracted a sheet of paper on which he had written everything he knew about General Jacques Lafitte.

'The general is fifty-four,' he told Gautier, 'and comes of a good family that is distantly related to the old ducal house of Lafitte-Chiramay. He was the youngest son and so he joined the army. As a young officer he served with distinction in the war against Prussia.'

'That can't have been difficult,' Gautier observed. 'In a war when the French army capitulated with ignominy, anyone who made even a token resistance must have served with distinction.'

'It's easy for those who are too young to remember to criticize,' Corbin said sharply. Like several others in the Sûreté he liked to remind Gautier from time to time that he had been made an inspector at an indecently early age. Then he continued, 'Lafitte married well: a Russian aristocrat with money, Natalie Bakalov. He's a member of the best clubs, including the Cercle Anglais and the Cercle Militaire; they have an hôtel particulier in Paris and a château in Provence.' He put the paper back into its folder and looked at Gautier. 'Why are you asking all this, Inspector?'

'It may have a bearing on the poisoning of Sophie Monterant.'

'My God! You're not suggesting that the general could possibly have been involved?'

'She was supposed to have been his mistress.'

'That's a different matter altogether.' Corbin looked almost hurt at even the suggestion that a man of good family might have stooped to poisoning.

'It's his wife I wish to talk with. Have you the address of their home in Paris.'

'I have, but you won't find Madame Lafitte there. She had a "crise des nerfs" a few months ago and the doctor sent her away.'

'To an asylum?'

'Certainly not! She's in the Maison de Santé of Dr Martin in Passy.'

'Ah!' Gautier exclaimed, teasing him. 'A rich man's asylum!'

5

THE TRAIN WHICH brought Marcel Pelotti back to Paris was
more than one hour late. Gautier spent the time in one of the
small cafés that faced the Gare de Lyon with the two policemen
who had been detailed to accompany him to the station. The evening had unexpectedly turned cold and damp, with a fine drizzle
that moistened the cobbles in the station forecourt till they glowed
in the light from the gas lamps.

One of the policemen said to Gautier as they drank their beer:
'Why is Pelotti being given this special treatment, Inspector?'

'What is special about it?'

'The director spoke to both of us before we left the Sûreté. He
told us that on no account are we to speak to the prisoner and that
if he speaks to us, we are to report what he says to the director
personally.'

'Perhaps the director is concerned for your personal safety,'
Gautier said jokingly. 'Isn't our friend Pelotti reputed to be an
expert with bombs?'

'Bombs indeed! I doubt whether he ever even saw one, let alone
exploded any.'

'He was a pimp,' the other policeman added. 'Show me the pimp
who has the stomach for violence.'

'It is said that he did not just deal in girls,' Gautier remarked.

'That's true and if you ask me it's the reason for all this secrecy.
It is common knowledge that a number of society ladies fancied
Pelotti enough to let him be their lover. Now people at the top are
afraid of what he might say, what names he might mention.'

'Who knows? Perhaps the wife of the Minister of Justice had
him as a lover.'

'You must be joking!' Gautier said, laughing. 'Have you ever seen the lady? She's well over sixty and bent double with rheumatism.'

'Maybe Pelotti is a contortionist in addition to all his other talents.'

At seven o'clock the three of them left the café and waited in the station by the platform where the train was due. Soon it arrived but it was not until all the other passengers had disembarked that Pelotti was brought off by his escort of an inspector and two policemen. Gautier wondered whether this was another of the precautions ordered by Courtrand.

One of the policemen was carrying a leather valise and the other a hat-box. Pelotti walked slightly in front of them, next to the inspector, dressed in a frock-coat, grey waistcoat and top hat. From the elegant cravat, held in place with a diamond pin, to the grey spats and highly polished elastic-sided boots, everything he was wearing would have been acceptable in style and cut in the most exclusive salons in Paris, except for the handcuffs at his wrists.

The inspector formally handed over his prisoner in the forecourt of the station where the horse-drawn police wagon stood waiting. The two men with Gautier took the valise and the hatbox and the inspector handed him a brown-paper package which had been securely tied with string and sealed at the knots.

'This contains the papers we found on the prisoner when he was arrested, as well as a false passport and money. It is for the personal attention of the director-general.'

'I understand.'

Gautier was locked in the wagon with Pelotti and the two policemen went to ride with the driver in the front. As the wagon moved off, the muffled sound of the horses' hooves struck up a monotonous and melancholy rhythm. Gautier looked at Pelotti curiously. The Italian seemed composed and self-assured, seeming in no way disturbed by the knowledge that he was on his way to long weeks in prison, hours of questioning, a trial and ultimately no doubt the guillotine.

'Any chance of my having a smoke?' Pelotti asked suddenly.

'I don't see why not; if you have anything to smoke.'

'Your colleague at the border allowed me to keep my cigars.'

With some difficulty, hampered by the handcuffs, the Italian took a leather cigar-case from his breast-pocket, extracted a cigar and bit off the end. Gautier found matches in his own pocket and held out a light.

'I don't suppose I'll be enjoying the luxury of expensive cigars much longer,' Pelotti remarked and when Gautier made no comment he added: 'Still, my luck had to run out eventually.'

'Luck?'

'Yes. All my life I've been lucky. Things have always gone right for me. And then that woman Lucie Bertron had to die.'

'You speak as though you didn't kill her?'

'I did, but not intentionally. Why should I? We had a very happy arrangement, Lucie and I.'

Gautier looked at him sceptically. 'Are you saying she broke her neck by accident.'

'Exactly that. It was an accident. Of course I was knocking her around at the time, but that was what Lucie liked. A lot of women enjoy being beaten.'

'A strange perversion!'

'Agreed, but then she was a strange woman, that Lucie. Bankers, dukes, politicians would pay 20,000 francs to go to bed with her, but that didn't satisfy Lucie. She had to have a man like me.'

'Perhaps she wanted to be the paymaster for a change, to call the tune.'

'I never took money from her, only presents. And I certainly didn't mean to kill her. I'd had a lot to drink, of course. We'd been out to dinner that night and she kept pressing drink on me, wine, champagne, cognac. She always said I was better in bed when I'd had a bit to drink. I hit her too hard, she fell badly and broke her neck. It was a chance in a thousand.'

'If that's what happened, why didn't you send for the police and tell them so?'

'Come, Inspector! Who would have believed me? Would you?'

'Probably not.'

'Well, there you are.'

43

They sat in silence for a time as the wagon trundled at a leisurely pace towards the Sûreté. Gautier found himself trying to decide in what category of criminal he should place Pelotti. He had learnt from experience that men took to crime for many reasons—greed, laziness, bravado. Some became criminals through force of circumstances and a small number because they were vicious and perverted and found pleasure in cruelty and violence. Pelotti, he decided, did not fall neatly into any classification. The Italian had a curious air of detachment and fatalism, not the fatalism of the superstitious but that of the philosopher.

'My life started when I was fourteen,' Pelotti remarked, as though he had sensed what Gautier might be thinking. 'My parents were peasants in Italy and put me out to work on a farm. The farmer's wife was thirty-four and vigorous, her husband an ailing, old man. For three years she used me, without showing me any favours, without giving me any reward. But she taught me one thing, that I had a way with women. She and the old man had saved up a bit of money and I knew where they kept it. So one day I helped myself, just what I calculated I had earned as a substitute husband, no more. I took the money, slipped over the border into France and lost myself in Marseille. That was the only real crime I have ever committed.'

'Didn't you live on women?'

'Yes, but who says that's a crime? Back home the women did the heavy work in the fields while the men sat drinking in cafés. Which is worse? Living on what a woman earns digging ditches all day or on what she earns in twenty minutes on her back?'

Gautier did not answer, for he had no wish to become involved in a discussion on the relationship between man and wife. The memory of the day when he had returned home to find that Suzanne had left him was too fresh and still posed too many unanswered questions about what a marriage should be. To change the subject, he held up the parcel which he had been given by Pelotti's escort.

'What's in this?' he asked facetiously. 'The manuscript of your memoirs?'

'No,' Pelotti replied, and added without bitterness: 'It was to be my future.'

'Money?'

'A thousand francs in gold, a letter of credit for 200,000 and quite a bit in notes.'

'If you didn't take money from women, how did you amass that fortune?'

This time it was Pelotti's turn to ignore a question. He glanced coldly at Gautier, as though the innuendo had offended him, then regained his composure and laughed. 'Never mind the money, my friend. As you'll see when you open it, that parcel also contains dynamite. No, not the kind that anarchists use, but something that will certainly cause an explosion in Paris.'

The police wagon had stopped and presently the doors were opened, showing that they were outside the Sûreté. Gautier and one of the policemen escorted Pelotti into the building and up to the office of the director-general on the first floor. No one seemed to take much interest in their arrival. Gautier had expected that a crowd of spectators and a few journalists would have been waiting either at the station or on the Quai des Orfèvres to see the infamous prisoner being brought back, but evidently the secret of Pelotti's arrest had been well kept.

Leaving the Italian and the policeman in the corridor, he went in to see Courtrand. The director was seated at his desk, talking to a tall man with thin features and bony hands, whom Gautier recognized as Judge Rolland. He realized that this probably meant that Rolland had been appointed the juge d'instruction in the matter of Lucie Bertron's death. The judge was known as a hard man who questioned prisoners as long and as mercilessly as the Inquisition.

'I have the prisoner Pelotti outside, Monsieur le Directeur,' Gautier told Courtrand.

'Good! Did he give you any trouble?'

'None at all.'

'What did the two of you talk about on the journey from the Gare de Lyon?' Judge Rolland asked.

'Pelotti told me about his childhood and of how a farmer's wife led him from the path of virtue.'

'Nothing more?'

'Only that he had killed Lucie Bertron by accident.'

45

'Some accident!' Courtrand exclaimed. 'She only had a broken neck.'

'It seems that being beaten up gave the woman Bertron sexual pleasure.'

The judge's nose wrinkled up in disgust. He was a man of high moral rectitude. 'These courtesans! Why society tolerates them, I simply cannot understand.'

'Did he mention any names?' Courtrand asked and Gautier could sense anxiety in the question.

'What sort of names?'

'Women who have been his mistresses.'

'Only Bertron—and the farmer's wife, of course.'

'That's something at least. You can send the scoundrel in now, Gautier.'

'Do you wish me to be present when you see him?'

'That won't be necessary. Just leave a man in the corridor outside in case he should turn violent.'

After carrying out these instructions, Gautier went upstairs to his own room where he found Surat waiting for him. His assistant was holding the box of chocolates which he had taken to the government laboratories that morning.

'What news from the chemists?' Gautier asked him.

'All the chocolates in the top layer had been poisoned; twenty-one in all.'

'How was it done?'

'Very skilfully. The chocolates were all filled with cream of different flavours. The poisoner carefully cut out a circular piece of the chocolate, extracted some of the cream, mixed it with a quantity of poison and put the mixture back into the chocolates. She then replaced the circular piece and applied a little warmth to melt the edges of the chocolate and thus conceal the join.'

'You speak as though the poisoner must have been a woman.'

'Only a woman would have had the patience. Don't they say that poison is a woman's weapon?'

Gautier smiled. 'The history books will tell you that a good many men have excelled at the art as well. What poison was used?'

46

'As the doctor thought, cyanide. The government chemist thought the doctor was clever to have detected it. Apparently the symptoms of death by cyanide are very similar to a heart attack.

'Dr Laradon was Madame Monterant's own physician, so he would have known if she had a history of heart trouble. Anyway she was a young woman.'

'When I arrived back from the laboratories,' Surat continued, 'they told me you were at the Gare de Lyon. So to fill in the time, I took the box of chocolates and showed it to Labiche, the chocolatiers.'

'That was sensible. What did they have to say?'

'They admitted that the box was one of theirs. It seems they bring out a new model every two months or so, decorated in a style to suit the season. Last autumn, for example, they had one decorated with pheasant feathers to mark the beginning of the shooting season. This particular box is their spring model, on sale about a month ago. But they turned up their noses at the chocolates, which they say are of poor quality and certainly not made by them.'

'I don't suppose they keep records giving the names of their customers.'

'No, but they do keep an order book. Almost all of the boxes of chocolates which they sell are not carried out of their shop, but ordered by wealthy customers who ask for them to be delivered, usually with a card or message, to the home of a friend or a relative or a mistress.'

'Did you ask them for a list of all the people who received a box like the one you're holding?'

'Yes, Patron. It will take them some time to compile because they sold more than 200.'

'Good. Perhaps you could pick it up from them tomorrow?'

Surat paused before he replied. He had the manner of a man who had news to report which he believed to be important and which he would enjoy reporting. Finally he said: 'Of course, but while I was there today I did glance quickly through the order book. I saw a name there which will interest you.'

Suddenly Gautier sensed what he was going to say, but he

47

decided not to spoil Surat's pleasure by guessing. So he merely asked: 'What name?'

'A box of the chocolates was ordered by General Jacques Lafitte; a very special order to be delivered with not only a letter, but a diamond bracelet placed inside. It was a gift to the singer, Clémentine Lyse.'

6

AS ALWAYS AT eleven o'clock at night, L'Attentat was crowded
to overflowing. Gautier was on the point of being turned away,
but eventually a small table was produced for him from the kitchen
and other patrons persuaded to move their chairs closer together
and make room for it.

When café-concerts had been introduced to Paris from
Marseille, they had simply been as the name suggested, cafés in
which entertainment of a kind was provided for the customers. In
a short time, however, to cater for a growing demand, a whole
range of different types of caf'conc's had come into being. At one
end of the scale there were huge establishments like the Eldorado,
which could seat 1,500 and which were to all intents and purposes
music-halls. There were also scores of smaller caf'conc's, each of
which the owner tried to invest with a distinctive character and
atmosphere of its own: caf'conc's like the Chat Noir where, in
addition to music, a shadow show was put on for the customers; the
Mirliton where Aristide Bruant, dressed in a black corduroy suit,
crimson shirt and black boots, greeted his well-to-do patrons with
insulting banter and then sang them his witty, cynical songs; the
Eden Concert, with its homely entertainment for the family; the
Rotonde, where one could find the anarchists, the nihilists, the
cubists and the drugtakers.

L'Attentat was a cellar café, unpretentious and even squalid in
appearance, with plain wooden tables and benches and a ceiling
so low that singers performing on the low platform which served
as a stage were afraid to raise their arms for fear of hitting it.
The gas jets which were used as footlights added their heat to a
room that was poorly ventilated and usually reeked of wine and
tobacco smoke. In spite of these discomforts, L'Attentat had

recently and suddenly become the most popular place of evening entertainment for the cultured and the discerning. Writers, poets and artists could be seen there every evening among the audience, together with a sprinkling of people from society, who wished to be thought intellectual and progressive.

Clémentine Lyse was only one of three well-known caf'conc' singers who were then appearing at L'Attentat. She gave one show at eleven-thirty, having already performed earlier in the evening at the Eldorado. Gautier had read in the newspapers that she was reputed to be the most highly-paid caf'conc' singer in France, earning 600 francs a night at the Eldorado and a further 300 for her performance at L'Attentat.

Singers of all kinds and a wide variety of songs were to be heard in the different establishments. For popular tastes, buxom women sang patriotic airs, comedians sang ballads full of smut with suggestive winks and grimaces, demure young ladies poured out romantic stories of love. There were also singing beggars, singing soldiers, singing clowns and even singing priests. Clémentine Lyse had built her reputation on songs that were in keeping with the realism in literature, that described with accuracy, and often with irony, life in the other Paris, the lives of working people, of petty criminals, of the out-of-work and the hopeless.

At precisely eleven-thirty that evening she came onto the makeshift stage of L'Attentat. She wore a long, beige dress, simply cut and without ornaments or jewellery. Her face, with high cheekbones and deepset eyes, seemed unnaturally pale, an effect which was heightened by the way she wore her hair, swept back from her face and tied at the back of her neck. The impression she gave was of a thin, gaunt woman in no way striking except for her intense and melancholy expression.

She waited for the audience to be silent and then began to sing. Her first song was 'A La Villette', one made famous several years previously by Bruant at the Mirliton. It was supposed to be sung by a young girl and described how she had fallen in love with one of the 'voyous' of Paris, a brash scoundrel living on his wits and on the edge of the law until inevitably he fell foul of it. The final verse of the song painted a picture of the last time she saw him:

La dernière fois que je l'ai vu,
Il avait l'torse à moitié nu,
Et le cou pris dans la Lunette
à la Villette.

The words were banal enough, but the way Clémentine Lyse sang them, totally without sentiment and with no more than a hint of poignant despair brought the scene vividly and uncomfortably to life. Gautier could almost see the boy, stripped to the waist, his neck held firmly in the frame at the bottom of the guillotine as the shining blade waited, poised above him. How many young men, he wondered, had died exactly like that before a stolid, unfeeling crowd outside the prison at La Rochette.

Clémentine Lyse sang four more songs, all of the same genre: songs of prostitutes and pimps, of drunkards and outcasts, of the old, the out-of-work and the homeless. Her voice lacked the melodious, vibrant quality of a true singer and for much of the time she did little more than recite her words in the style of a 'diseuse', but her delivery had a powerful simplicity and when she raised her voice to sing the final, evocative words of a song, the effect was strangely moving.

When the end of her performance was approaching, Gautier took one of his official cards and wrote on the back of it:

Mademoiselle,
I would be grateful if you would do me the courtesy of allowing me to speak to you for a few minutes after your performance.
Jean-Paul Gautier.

He placed the card in one of the small envelopes which he always carried—it was often diplomatic to conceal his identity from waiters and domestic servants—and addressed the envelope to Clémentine Lyse. Then he gave the envelope to a waiter and asked him to take it to the singer as soon as she left the stage.

Her final song received much more applause than he had expected. The audience which L'Attentat attracted, intellectuals and those with pretentions to good taste, was in his experience not

51

only highly critical but also reluctant to display enthusiasm. He found himself wondering whether it was her style of singing the audience admired or whether her songs of poverty and misery in some way stirred their social conscience.

A short time after she had left the café by a door at the back of the room, the waiter who had taken his message came and told Gautier that Mademoiselle Lyse would see him in her dressing-room. He followed the man through the same door as the singer had used and then through a small, hot and singularly dirty kitchen. At the far end of the kitchen were two more doors, one marked 'Toilette' and the other 'Artistes'. The waiter knocked on the second of the two and ushered Gautier through.

Clémentine Lyse was sitting with her back to the door in front of a small mirror that was perched on a packing-case to serve as a dressing-table. The room was evidently used by all the performers appearing at L'Attentat, for a man's frock-coat hung on the back of the door while a vast, purple dress, obviously the costume of a lady of massive proportions, was draped untidily over a second packing-case. A screen behind which the artistes could change in some privacy had also been squeezed into the tiny room.

'It's good of you to see me, Mademoiselle,' Gautier began.

She turned to face him. 'What can I do for you, Inspector?' Although her voice was calm and assured, her eyes were watchful.

In front of the gas lights of the stage, her face had seemed to be completely without make-up. Now that she was taking it off, Gautier could see that she had used cosmetics skilfully to create the almost unhealthy pallor which had been so effective on the stage. Free of powder and cream, her complexion was healthy with a slight tan, her features no longer gaunt, but rounded and soft.

'I am making enquiries into the death of Sophie Monterant,' Gautier told her.

'Indeed?'

'You had heard that she was poisoned last night?'

'Even if the whole of Paris has not heard that, everyone in the theatre has.'

'I will speak frankly, Mademoiselle,' Gautier began.

'An English friend of mine once observed that whenever a

52

Frenchman announces that he is going to speak frankly, one may confidently expect a monstrous lie.'

'This is no lie. I have come because we have been told that you might have hated Sophie Monterant enough to have killed her.'

She looked away and for a time made no reply. Then still without looking at Gautier she said quietly: 'I see that you are a man of your word, Monsieur, though your frankness might be mistaken by some for brutality. Yes, it's true I hated Sophie Monterant.'

'But you did not kill her?'

Her self-control suddenly collapsed, stretched beyond breaking point. She turned on him, two scarlet patches of anger on her cheekbones. 'Mother of God! All my life that woman haunted me, mocked me, crushed me! Now that she's dead at last, is there to be no relief?'

Even if there had been a reply to her question, Gautier would not have made it. When a woman could no longer restrain her emotions, one learnt more by listening than by talking. He could see that Clémentine Lyse would need no prompting to talk.

'Oh, yes, Inspector,' she continued bitterly, 'one might say that I had many reasons for hating Monterant. Everything that I should have had in my professional life she took, not because she had more talent but because she had family influence and connections and, when those failed, because her body was more desirable than mine—and more available.'

'Most people would say that you have had a greater success than Madame Monterant.'

'Success? How does one measure it? Let us go back a dozen years or more, Inspector, when I first met Monterant. We both applied for places at the Conservatoire at the same time. She was a girl of good education with well-to-do, bourgeois parents; I an illegitimate child who had worked since I was six years old, helping my mother to scratch a living for the two of us. Do you know what it's like to work sixteen hours a day to earn fifty centimes, Inspector? Or to sing and dance in the streets in the hope that some passer-by might throw you a sou? I had worked for my chance, having earned enough to pay for lessons in diction and acting and having rehearsed my examination piece a thousand times. Sophie came beautifully dressed, smiling and mincing and because her family knew the examiners, she even had the temerity not to prepare a proper piece. Instead she just recited an Aesop fable. Yet we were both accepted and with equal recognition. And during our two years of study, it was I who won the praises and the admiration of our professors and fellow-students, but who won the prizes? Sophie, of course.'

Unlike the journalist, Cros, she seemed unaware that justice was blindfolded. A childhood in the streets of Paris, Gautier reflected, should have taught her, as fifteen years enforcing the law had taught him, that life seldom distributed rewards where they were merited. He said nothing.

Meanwhile she had risen from her chair and gone behind the screen. As she changed her dress she continued speaking. 'As we were graduating from the Conservatoire, the Comédie-Française wished to add a young actress to their pensionnaires. Was Sophie given the contract rather than me on account of her acting ability, do you suppose, or because that ageing lecher, the Minister of Beaux-arts, interceded on her behalf?'

She came out from behind the screen, now wearing a turquoise dress with a high waist and a low neck-line. Her dark hair had been untied and hung to her shoulders, completing the transformation in her appearance. Now she was no longer a gaunt, consumptive woman, but an attractive beauty dressed by Worth or Poiret, indistinguishable from the many rich and elegant creatures to be found in Paris's gratin.

Some of her anger appeared to have evaporated and she said to Gautier: 'Did you ever see Monterant perform?'

'Only once. By coincidence it was at the Châtelet last night.'

'In *La Dame aux Camélias*? What did you think of her?'

'The play was trite and sentimental, but I was impressed by her acting.'

'At least you're honest. And what was your opinion of my singing tonight?'

Gautier paused to search for the right words. 'Moving, powerful and very effective. And what you sang was much closer to life than anything Dumas fils ever wrote.'

She seemed satisfied with his answer. Gathering together the combs, cosmetics and pots of cream she had been using, she put them and the beige dress, neatly folded, into a small valise. 'My carriage is waiting outside. Would you be kind enough to escort me to it, Inspector?'

'Willingly.'

Gautier took the valise and followed her through the kitchen to a back door which opened on to a flight of steps which in turn led to the street, where a carriage with driver and footman was waiting. A crowd of about fifty people had gathered on the pavement outside the café and when Clémentine Lyse appeared several of them cheered and applauded.

'Quite a demonstration of affection!' Gautier remarked.

'This is nothing. Sometimes there are hundreds outside the Eldorado.'

He escorted her to the carriage where the footman had already opened the door for her. One or two women in the crowd reached out and tried to touch her as she passed, either to feel the rich silk of her dress or perhaps in the hope that some of her wealth and good fortune might rub off on to them.

She paused by the door to the carriage, one foot on the step. 'I'm sorry that I haven't been of much help to you, Monsieur Gautier.'

'This was only a start. Perhaps I may come and trouble you with more questions another time?'

'Certainly. But what questions?'

'About the people who knew Sophie Monterant. Others who might have hated her.' He smiled, 'Or loved her. Men like General Jacques Lafitte. They say he was her lover.'

'So I believe.'

'What sort of man is he? Passionate? Jealous? Violent?'

She seemed surprised at his questions. 'How would I know, Monsieur Gautier? I have never met the general.'

7

THE MAISON DE SANTÉ of Dr Martin was a large house in a quiet, tree-lined street in Passy. It had been built some years previously by a merchant who had made a fortune in the period following the war with Germany, as his home. There was nothing in the façade of the house to suggest that it was not still the private residence of a wealthy family except for the bars on the upper-floor windows, which had been put there not to imprison the inmates of the establishment, but to prevent deranged patients from attempting suicide.

The manservant who opened the door showed Gautier into a study where the chief resident physician, a Dr Préviot, was working at his desk. The proprietor of the Maison de Santé, Professor Martin, was now a celebrity in Paris, much in demand among duchesses and rich foreigners and he only visited his sanatorium for occasional consultations and for meetings with his accountant.

Dr Préviot was a middle-aged man, thoroughly respectable in his dress and manner, with a waxed moustache and thinning hair which he spread out to cover as much of his skull as possible and fixed carefully in place with pomade. After introducing himself, Gautier explained that he was making enquiries concerning the death of the actress Sophie Monterant.

'And how can we help, Inspector?' Préviot asked.

'Is it true that you have among your patients the wife of General Jacques Lafitte?'

The doctor smiled. 'Who tried to shoot Madame Monterant eighteen months ago? Yes, she is here.'

'You know about that incident?'

'Of course. It is a part of Madame Lafitte's case history. One might even say that it was the first symptom of the illness which eventually brought her to us.'

'I have to ask you this question, Dr Préviot. Do you think it is possible that Madame Lafitte might have wished to kill Madame Monterant again?'

'What you really want to know is whether she had any part in the actress's death.'

'Yes.'

'How and where did she die?'

Briefly Gautier described how Sophie Monterant had been killed and at what time of day she had died. An inner sense of caution prevented him from saying what poison had been used and how it had been put into the chocolates. Doctors were not always on the side of the law.

'I cannot say,' Préviot commented, when Gautier had finished speaking, 'that it would have been impossible for Madame Lafitte to have been involved in this crime. Our patients are not prisoners. They have contacts outside the sanatorium. People come to visit them. Some of them are well enough to go into Paris on their own from time to time.'

'And has Madame Lafitte been into the city recently?'

'Not often. Two or three times during the last month. But in my opinion it's extremely unlikely that even if she had the opportunity, she would wish to kill Sophie Monterant.'

'Why do you say that?'

'Her husband's infidelities are no longer preoccupying her. I doubt if she even thinks about them. They are certainly not a factor in her illness at the present time.'

'Are you sure of that?'

Préviot smiled, sensing that Gautier was not convinced by what he had said. 'Don't rely on my opinion, Inspector. Why don't you go and talk to Madame Lafitte and judge for yourself?'

'You have no objection?'

'None at all. She's not insane, nor even deranged, you know. For most of the time she is completely rational in what she does and will converse sensibly and logically.'

'Then why is she here?'

'To protect her from herself. Madame Lafitte is suffering from acute melancholia and her fits of depression can be dangerous. Come, let's see if we can find her. At this time of the morning she should be in the garden.'

The garden behind the house was much larger than one would have expected, stretching back to a small copse of trees that might have been an orchard in the days when Passy was a country village. Shrubs and climbing plants on trellis-work had been cleverly arranged to create sheltered areas where patients could walk or sit and feel themselves alone, although one sensed that wherever they might be there would always be eyes watching.

They found Madame Lafitte sitting on a rustic wooden seat in one of those secluded places. She was a large, unshapely woman with dark eyes and untidy hair, who would have seemed clumsy had it not been for the drawn, fragile look of ill-health in her features. Dr Préviot introduced Gautier to her, explained the purpose of his visit and then left the two of them alone together.

'So Sophie Monterant is dead?' Madame Lafitte asked.

'Yes. Hadn't you heard?'

She made no reply to his question. Instead she said: 'Poor Jacques. She has died too late. If I had killed her when I wished to, he would have had something left—his illusions and what's more important to him, his pride. As it is he has nothing.'

'Do you know who might have killed her?'

Again she ignored his question but went on speaking, dreamily, looking not at Gautier but into the distance as though she were thinking aloud: 'His love for her was like a disease. He knew she was using him, using his social position and influence to further her ambitions, but he was even prepared to accept that. He could never understand that sooner or later she would abandon him for a man of even greater social distinction.'

'Who was that?'

'The theatre is changing, Inspector. Do you know that not all that many years ago actors were considered degenerate and immoral? Why, the Church once even refused a famous actor, Phillipe, a sacred burial because of the parts he had played. Now actresses are accepted in society.'

'I read somewhere,' Gautier commented, 'that an actress can

58

gain entrance to the highest social circles only by leaving her bedroom door open.'

'They say that Sophie Monterant was a regular guest at the Limousin home.'

'Limousin?'

Madame Lafitte looked at him, with curiosity, as though she had only just become aware of his presence. 'The Comte and Comtesse de Limousin. They have a magnificent house on Avenue du Bois de Boulogne. It was the comte whom poor Jacques challenged to a duel.'

'Did they actually fight?'

'Oh, yes. A month ago. With épées. Jacques has never mentioned it, so I suppose it was another humiliation.'

Though the fighting of duels had long been illegal, members of the upper crust still believed them to be the only way of settling differences between gentlemen. So from time to time duels were fought, supposedly in great secrecy and in accordance with an elaborate ceremonial laid down by tradition. The police usually turned a blind eye to these affairs which invariably ended in nothing more dramatic than a graze, which the recipient was able to wear, heavily bandaged, as a badge of courage.

'Do you believe in God's punishment?' Madame Lafitte asked unexpectedly.

'Yes, I suppose I do.'

'This is my punishment.'

'For attempting to kill Sophie Monterant?'

'Of course not! There was no crime in that.' She looked at Gautier in mild exasperation as though he were being unreasonably obtuse. 'For leaving my country. For selfishness. I came to Paris because I wanted a gay and easy life: dinner parties, balls, the theatre and a handsome husband. For these trivial things I abandoned my country and its poor, unhappy people. And all I have found is my own unhappiness.'

Gautier said nothing. After a brief moment of contact she seemed to have retreated once more into a monologue. As she was speaking her face gradually took on an expression of intense sadness.

'And there's worse to come,' she said slowly. 'Every night I

dream of a disaster that is going to overtake the Russian people.'
'What kind of disaster?'
'That is never made clear. An earthquake perhaps, or a plague or a bloody civil war. Thousands will die. I awake from these dreams sobbing at what I have seen and knowing that they are going to come true, knowing that there is nothing I can do to prevent them, knowing that I share the guilt for them.'

She stopped speaking. Gautier tried to say a few words that might reassure her, but she did not seem to hear him. Her body began to shake with silent, convulsive sobs. He left her sitting on the garden seat, alone in a private world, tortured by an anguish of her own making. As he moved away across the grass, he found himself walking on tip-toe.

Later that same day Gautier knocked at the door of a house far more imposing than Dr Martin's Maison de Santé. It was only one of several magnificent residences in the Avenue du Bois, a broad, tree-flanked avenue which led from Etoile to the Bois de Boulogne. The house had been built six years previously by Comte Edmond de Limousin and while it was neither as magnificent nor as costly as the Palais Rose, the home of Comte Boni de Castellane, which stood only a short distance away and which had been modelled on the Petit Trianon in Versailles, it was none the less large and opulent. When Gautier arrived a carriage with a team of four white horses was standing in the entrance drive. A coachman and two liveried footmen stood waiting by it, their faces wearing the resigned and patient expressions of those who wait more often than they work.

The front door was opened by a manservant in silver and green livery, who led him up a broad staircase to a room on the first floor where a girl received him. She was about eighteen, fair-haired and one of the most beautiful girls Gautier had ever seen and introduced herself as the secretary to the Comtesse de Limousin. When Gautier told her it was the comte he wished to see, she left him a few moments and returned to say that the comte was not available, but the comtesse would see the Inspector.

They went together through a vast drawing-room, large enough to take at least a hundred people, along a panelled picture gallery hung with portraits of the comte's ancestors and into a smaller, more informal reception room where the comtesse was waiting.

To Gautier's surprise she was sitting on the carpet in front of an artist's easel on which there stood a portrait of her. The painting was strikingly unusual, executed almost entirely in black and white and shades of grey and showed the comtesse in a black, amazonian riding-habit.

She must have noticed him looking at the canvas, for she said: 'What do you think of my portrait, Inspector? It was painted by a brilliant young American artist, Romaine Brooks.'

'It scarcely flatters you, Madame.'

Even as he spoke the conventional response, he wondered if he was being truthful. In the portrait, the comtesse seemed sombre and severe, but even so not unattractive. Facing him he saw a woman with a long face and a big, hawkish nose, wearing a dress made out of russet coloured, loosely-woven material, which looked as though it had been run up in a hurry by enthusiastic but unskilful home dressmakers. Her hair hung straight to her shoulders with a broad band tied round her forehead that only needed a feather to give her the look of an Indian squaw.

'Evidently the inspector sees some beauty in my features which escaped the notice of Romaine Brooks,' said the comtesse, laughing, to her beautiful secretary.

'My purpose in coming to your home,' Gautier said, mildly irritated, 'was to speak with your husband.'

'That's out of the question, I'm afraid. As usual he's asleep. Haven't you heard, Inspector, that the comte's favourite pastime is sleep?'

'No, Madame.'

'He sleeps late every morning, again in the afternoon and has a short nap before dinner. Why, he has even fallen asleep at the concerts which we hold here in our house, at dinner parties, at the opera. A gentleman friend of his swears he once saw Edmond asleep on a horse riding through the Bois de Boulogne.'

The beautiful young secretary, who had gone and sat down on a chair behind her employer, laughed girlishly. Gautier realized that he was not going to be offered a seat.

61

'Why do you wish to see my husband?' the comtesse asked.

'To talk to him about the duel which he is reported to have fought with General Jacques Lafitte.'

'Oh, come, Monsieur Gautier! Senior inspectors of the Sûreté don't concern themselves with the childish games that grown men play in the park at dawn. You're really here to talk to him about the death of the actress Sophie Monterant.'

'According to our information, the two events could be related.'

'Surely you don't imagine that my husband could be involved in the killing of Madame Monterant?'

'I have no reason to believe so,' Gautier admitted.

The comtesse stared at him and then burst out laughing. 'How naïve I'm being! It's not my husband you suspect of poisoning the beautiful Monterant, but me!'

Although her French was fluent, grammatically correct and cultured, one could detect in it a German accent. The comtesse, it was well-known in Paris, was German by birth, the rich daughter of an armaments manufacturer whose first marriage had been to the son of the head of the largest dairy produce company in France. This union had been ended by the untimely death of the comtesse's first husband, which left her childless, alone and enormously wealthy. She had then married Comte Edmond de Limousin, a man ten years younger than herself, of an ancient family agreed to be better bred than all the royal houses of Europe, extravagantly handsome and extravagantly in debt.

'That's right, isn't it?' the comtesse continued. 'You do believe I may have had a hand in killing Sophie Monterant.'

'Did you, Madame?'

'For what reason, pray? Jealousy? Monsieur Gautier, I wonder if you will be able to understand what I am going to tell you. My husband, Edmond, is thirty-eight years old, ten years younger than me. I did not marry him to, if I may paraphrase Shakespeare, fan the bellows of an ageing woman's lust. My main interest in life, as you may discern, is culture.' She pointed at the room around her, at the pictures and the furniture and the ornaments. 'I like to be surrounded by beautiful things, by beautiful and artistic people.'

'With your wealth, Madame,' Gautier said drily, 'that should not be difficult.'

'So far as material objects are concerned that is true. But what use is art without people to appreciate it? Our house, Inspector, has become the centre of avant-garde culture in Paris. People come here to hear new musicians play, to hear new poets declaim their verses, to see new paintings and sculptures. Without a husband, all my wealth could not have created a salon like mine. As you must be aware, unmarried women, even widows, are not respectable in Paris society.'

While the comtesse had been speaking, another girl, as young and almost as beautiful as the one who sat listening to their conversation, had come into the room. She was carrying a hairbrush and without speaking she knelt down behind the comtesse and began to brush her hair.

'Of course my husband has mistresses,' the comtesse continued. 'Sophie Monterant was almost certainly one of them. But why should I mind? She was a great improvement on some he has had in the past, I can tell you: ballet dancers, circus riders; one was even a little milliner, I seem to remember.'

'Had you ever met Madame Monterant?'

'Certainly. She has been a guest in our house more than once. I liked her.'

'Has your husband by any chance ever provided finance for her plays?'

'Yes. He was one of the backers for her latest production.' The comtesse looked at Gautier mockingly. 'No, Monsieur Gautier, neither my husband nor I can really be cast in the rôle of poisoner.'

'I would still like to speak to your husband, Madame.'

'I don't know how that can be arranged. Frankly, even if you were to call when he was at home and awake, he would almost certainly refuse to see a mere inspector. My husband has a great regard for protocol. He would expect the Director of the Sûreté or even the Prefect of Police to be the one to come and see him.'

'It might be necessary for me to use the force of law and insist.'

'That would be tiresome and undignified.' The comtesse thought

63

about the matter for a time. 'I'd like to help you, Inspector. Why don't we do this in a civilised way? Come to our house tomorrow evening as a guest. We're having a reception in honour of a brilliant young pianist who is to play for us. If you come I will arrange an opportunity for you to speak to my husband. He could scarcely refuse in those circumstances.'

'Thank you. That is kind of you, Madame. I accept.'

'Good. Bring your wife, Monsieur Gautier. She might enjoy it.'

'Unfortunately my wife and I are separated.'

'Poor man! Then bring a friend.'

The comtesse's secretary got up to show him out and Gautier realized that the interview was at an end. He inclined his head to show that he understood and the comtesse said: 'Till tomorrow, then. Oh and we'll be wearing evening dress of course.'

8

THE SCENE IN the office of the Director-General that afternoon reminded Gautier of one of the grandiose paintings by the established artists of the day: Napoleon in his tent on the eve of a famous battle, planning his strategy for the morrow with his generals. Courtrand had assembled the senior inspectors of the Sûreté for a meeting, with his personal assistant to take notes and issue written instructions to all concerned in due course.

'Messieurs,' Courtrand told his staff pompously, 'I have called you together because I need your assistance in a matter of importance. I must have results and I must have them quickly.'

None of the inspectors was surprised at the summons to the director's office. It was not often that Courtrand took personal charge of an investigation, but when he did it invariably meant a general disruption of work for all senior staff, as they were required to drop whatever they were doing and to concentrate their energies on helping him.

'This morning,' Courtrand told them, 'the prisoner Pelotti was examined by Judge Rolland and myself. When he was arrested on the Italian border, he had a large sum of money in his possession. What we have now to establish as a matter of urgency is how he acquired that money.'

'Do you believe he might have stolen it?' one of the inspectors asked.

'Not in cash. The sum is too large. If Pelotti had robbed a bank we would have heard about it. He claims the money is his by right, his savings from the presents given to him by his lady friends over several years. My own view is that it represents the proceeds from the sale of jewellery which he stole from his mistress, Lucie Bertron, and perhaps from other women.'

Opening a folder which lay on the desk in front of him, Courtrand took out several copies of a list and handed them round to the inspectors. He said: 'Lucie Bertron's maid helped us to compile a list of her jewellery, none of which was to be found in the apartment after her death. The principal item is a pearl necklace, said to have been given to her by the King of Spain and insured for 200,000 francs.'

Courtrand told one inspector that he wanted to have the jewellery traced as quickly as possible. Policemen were to be sent, armed with copies of the list, to make enquiries at all the jewellers of Paris, starting with the establishments of dubious reputation which were known or suspected to be receivers of stolen property.

'Don't allow your men to be fobbed off with evasive answers,' he added. 'They must be prepared to be rough if necessary. Let the jewellers know that this is a matter of murder.'

The second inspector was then given an assignment, which was to find out where and in what company Pelotti had spent the two weeks between the death of Lucie Bertron and his arrest on the night train to Italy. No one, not even Pelotti, he pointed out, could disappear completely and without trace in Paris. He must have slept somewhere, eaten somewhere, been sheltered by someone. The inspector was to select a squad of men to invade the dunghill of the underworld, visiting the most disreputable cafés, questioning prostitutes and pimps, looking for informers.

Finally Courtrand turned to Gautier. 'Yours is the easiest task,' he said, 'and one in which you will not need help. I have chosen you for it because you are already involved in another affair. I want you to go to the bank of Gaston Merx et fils.'

'In Place Vendôme?'

'Precisely. When he was arrested, Pelotti had a letter of credit from the bank for 200,000 francs. The document is almost certainly a forgery, but the bank should be able to confirm that.'

Courtrand then took from the folder a bunch of photographs, which he handed to Gautier, telling him to keep one for himself and to divide the remainder between the other two inspectors.

'These will help identify Pelotti. He was carrying a false passport and has probably been using a false name.'

The photograph showed Pelotti dressed in a morning coat, standing in the stilted pose that was commonly adopted by gentlemen for portraits or when they faced a camera, with a silver-topped cane in one hand and a top hat in the other.

'Believe it or not,' Courtrand said angrily, 'this photograph was taken by Nadar, the society photographer. Is there no limit to this scoundrel's megalomania?'

The briefing was concluded. In the corridor outside Courtrand's office one of Gautier's fellow inspectors remarked: 'I can't see the urgency, or even the need, to find out where Pelotti got the money they found on him. Hasn't he admitted killing the woman, Bertron?'

'He's claiming the killing was an accident,' Gautier replied. 'If that story is believed, then he might get away with a prison sentence. But if it can be proved that he took her jewellery after killing her . . .' He left the sentence unfinished but added: 'Courtrand is determined that Pelotti won't escape the guillotine.'

The premises of Gaston Merx et fils on the north-east corner of Place Vendôme facing the Ritz Hotel, reminded Gautier more of a church than a bank. There was no sound of clinking coins, no ledgers to be seen and the staff spoke in hushed whispers as though money, like God, was to be revered and worshipped but not seen.

A Monsieur Oscar Grout, one of the firm's partners and the son-in-law of the founder, received Gautier in a beautifully furnished office. He was a balding man with the figure of an ageing wrestler and quick, inquisitive eyes. After they had exchanged the usual Gallic courtesies, Gautier produced Pelotti's letter of credit from his pocket.

'A letter of credit made out by your bank for a very substantial sum of money has come into the possession of the Sûreté.'

'May I see it?'

Gautier handed him the letter and Grout read it through carefully. As he was doing so, Gautier commented: 'It may well be a forgery of course, Monsieur.'

'No, it's perfectly genuine. See, I signed it myself.'

'It's made out in the name of a Georges Auguste. Do you know the gentleman?'

67

'Of course. Monsieur Auguste has banked with us for several years.'

'Then the letter must have been stolen from him.'

Grout shook his head. 'I doubt that very much, Inspector. Who would steal it? A letter of credit is worthless, except to the person in whose name it has been made out.'

Improbable as it might seem, there was only one logical explanation left. Gautier passed his photograph of Pelotti across to the banker. 'Do you know this man, Monsieur Grout?'

'Certainly. That's Monsieur Auguste.'

'And how long did you say he has been banking with your firm?'

'Without checking our records, I could not say exactly. Four years perhaps; at least three.'

'It will come as a shock to you, Monsieur, I am sure, to learn that Georges Auguste is better known to the police as Marcel Pelotti, a successful criminal, and that he is now in our custody suspected of killing a courtesan named Lucie Bertron.'

Grout was horror-struck. He looked as though he had just heard that the Paris Bourse had fallen or the Rothschilds been declared bankrupt. 'That cannot possibly be true!'

'I'm afraid it is.'

'And our bank accepted him as a client!'

'You're not the only people he has deceived, Monsieur. Pelotti is a plausible rogue.'

'Think of the disgrace!' Grout took out a handkerchief and dabbed his lips, which were twitching nervously. 'We are bankers to society, even to royalty. Who will ever respect our judgement again?'

'Your other clients need not necessarily know of this affair.'

'Do you really mean that?' Hope flared like a beacon in the banker's eyes.

'Certainly. It is not the policy of the Sûreté that innocent people should be involved in scandals. If you are prepared to help us, I will do what I can to see that your bank is not named in any process.'

'We'll give you all the help we can, that goes without saying, Inspector. What do you want to know?'

'Tell me how he came to be banking with you, the kind of funds he had at his disposal. His banking history, if you like.'

'I'll need to refresh my memory.'

Leaving Gautier alone in the office, Grout went away and returned a minute or two later carrying a folder tied with red tape. Gautier remembered the almost identical folders in which Courtrand's assistant, Corbin, kept his files of information on important people. Was it by an irony of symbolism, he wondered, that the secrets of men's achievements and of their fortunes and of their loves, the things that mattered most to them, should always be lodged in the same commonplace, anonymous folders casually secured with the same anonymous, official tape.

Thumbing through the file, Grout told him that Monsieur Georges Auguste had come to the bank four years and eight months previously with an introduction from a former German ambassador and a reference from a German bank. Auguste had explained that he was German by birth, but likely to be resident in Paris for several years and asked Gaston Merx et fils to handle his financial affairs. The partner who had interviewed him had not thought to check the reference. Was not the man tastefully dressed and well-mannered? Did he not produce a gilt-edged business card? Had he not appeared to be on familiar terms with members of the Prussian court? More important still, had he not immediately deposited a respectable sum of money with the bank?

Gautier sighed inwardly. Even bankers, it seemed, were vulnerable to the most elementary tricks of the professional swindler. 'Did he keep large sums with you?' he asked Grout.

'No, not exceptionally large. Just the sort of funds a gentleman would need to maintain a comfortable standard of life in Paris.'

'But he had enough to cover this substantial letter of credit?'

Grout spread his hands in a gesture as ancient as the money-lender's art. 'Only when we issued it. Two weeks ago, Monsieur Auguste, or whatever his name is, came and told us he was leaving Paris and would be living for some time in Italy. He said it was his intention to sell the furniture in his apartment, which was not suitable for the Italian climate, and was rather concerned that he might not be able to effect a sale before he left France. We agreed that in this eventuality we would handle the matter for him.'

'But a few days ago he received an offer for it in cash?'

'How did you know? Yes, he came and deposited a large sum and asked us to arrange a letter of credit, negotiable in Italy.'

'And a thousand francs in gold?'

'No. We did not supply him with that.'

Gautier took the letter of credit and the photograph back from Grout and returned them to his pocket. 'What we would like to know is where he really acquired this small fortune in cash. It certainly wasn't from the sale of furniture.'

'There I cannot help you, Inspector.'

'It doesn't matter. We'll find out in due course. But you were not suspicious that he might be fleeing the country when he came to you?'

'I still find it hard to believe that this was his intention. After all he didn't even close his account with us.' Grout checked with a balance sheet in his folder. 'He still has 17,081 francs deposited here. Not a sum that anyone would abandon lightly.'

'No,' Gautier agreed. 'The interest on that might well keep him in cigars for the rest of his life.'

9

AT SEVEN O'CLOCK next morning Gautier was at Sûreté headquarters. Although he was as usual one of the earliest to arrive,
there was already a message waiting for him, taken by one of the
clerks on night duty. A lady had telephoned, he was told, demanding to see the inspector that morning. No, she had refused to give
her name. The inspector was to be at the entrance to Parc Monceau
in Rue Rembrandt at no later than nine o'clock. The lady would
see him there. She had repeated the instructions, stressing that
Inspector Gautier must be at the park without fail. What she had
to say to him was of the greatest importance.

As he went up to his office to write a report for the director on
his visit to Gaston Merx et fils, Gautier wondered who the lady
caller might be. His first thought was that it was Sophie Monterant's
maid, Françoise, ready to offer another name as her mistress's
killer. Then he reflected that a humble countrywoman would never
have the temerity to summon a police inspector in that peremptory
fashion.

Recalling his encounter with the Comtesse de Limousin the
previous day, he began to believe, without any logical reason, that
it was she who wished to meet him again, alone and in secret.
Then he remembered Madame Lafitte. She surely must be the one.
The way the message had been delivered, the choice of meeting
place, the urgency in the instructions were all symptomatic of an
unsettled mind.

After finishing his report, which he would leave for Courtrand,
who seldom arrived at the Sûreté before ten in the morning, he
sent for Surat and gave him two assignments to carry out that
morning. The first was to call at the chocolatiers, Labiche, for the
list which they had promised to provide of people to whom their

spring boxes of chocolates had been delivered. The second was to visit the Châtelet theatre.

So far Gautier had concentrated his enquiries about Sophie Monterant's death to those people with whom she had had close personal relationships. He realized that it would be unwise to overlook her professional life. People of the theatre, actors, playwrights, producers, were a strange breed, leading irregular and artificial lives and becoming so practised in the art of simulating strong emotions that they often became unable to distinguish between the real and the counterfeit in their own feelings. Passions, jealousies and violent quarrels became part of their lives. People in Paris still recalled how Sarah Bernhardt had gone, raging with fury and armed with a dagger and a riding-whip, to the apartment of another actress, Marie Colombier, who had just published a scurrilous parody of Bernhardt's tour of America. In the same vein, more recently, the poet Maurice Maeterlinck had beaten Claude Debussy over the shoulders with a stick, enraged at an imagined slight to his mistress, Georgette Leblanc.

In Gautier's opinion it was quite likely that Sophie Monterant, by what he had heard of her behaviour and read in her diary, could have provoked similar passions and jealousies. He told Surat: 'In the article which it published about Monterant, *Figaro* mentioned the dunghill of scandal on which she had built her career. It's time we raked over the muck-heap to see what we can discover.'

Surat, he knew, would handle the task quietly and efficiently. He was a man of friendly, sympathetic disposition, in whom even strangers would quickly confide. Over a glass of wine or a marc, he would learn much from the little people of the theatre: stagehands, attendants and dressers.

When he had finished explaining to Surat what he wished him to do, Gautier left the Sûreté and took an omnibus from Rue de Rivoli to Boulevard Haussmann. It was the same route as he followed two days previously. Was it just coincidence, he wondered, that the woman who wished to see him had suggested an assignation only a short walk from Sophie Monterant's apartment.

There was no one waiting at the entrance to Parc Monceau when he reached Rue Rembrandt. At that time of day few people were to be seen in the streets in the district. Those who worked for a

living had already started to, and those who had no need to had
not yet emerged from their homes. As he waited, one or two
servants passed, mainly women on errands for their mistresses.
Gautier looked at each one, wondering whether perhaps a woman
who wished to meet him secretly might not come dressed as a
servant to disguise herself.

Ten minutes had passed and he was beginning to believe that
he might have been brought there for a hoax, when a carriage drew
to a halt on the corner of Rue Rembrandt and Rue Murillo. The
coachman, seeing him waiting there, beckoned and Gautier walked
across.

'The mistress wants you to join her inside,' the coachman said,
pointing downwards towards the carriage door. 'Climb in.'

Gautier did as the man said and inside the carriage found
Clémentine Lyse waiting for him. She was wearing a dark grey
cloak with a black hat and gloves and her face was pale and taut.
He sat down opposite her and she gave him a curt nod to acknow-
ledge his arrival. At the same time the carriage began to move
forward.

'Where are we going?' Gautier asked.

Ignoring his question she looked at him and he could see anger
and frustration in her eyes, but when she spoke her voice was quiet
and controlled. 'Tell me, Inspector Gautier, is it the policy of the
Sûreté to play a double game?'

'What do you mean?'

'When you came to see me the night before last, you said you
were speaking frankly.'

'And I did.'

'But not so frankly as to say you had taken the newspapers into
your confidence and that *Le Matin* would be naming me as the
person who poisoned Sophie Monterant.'

'Surely they didn't mention your name?'

'Who else could be a caf'conc' singer with the initials CL?'

'I'm sorry about that, but I am not responsible for whatever
they may have published.'

'No? Your denials are wasted, Inspector. I just cannot believe
you.' Her voice grew louder, her face inflamed and he could see
that an emotion stronger than anger was affecting her. 'Do you

realize what these accusations can do to me? Are you deliberately trying to ruin my career?' She paused, seemingly on the edge of tears. 'Last night at L'Attentat I was booed. I, Clémentine Lyse, whom thousands pack the Eldorado to see perform, was booed!'

'Because of a newspaper story?'

'Why else? The audience at L'Attentat are intellectuals and the theatre is their first love. They come to watch me after the theatre just to prolong the evening. To them I am onion soup at Les Halles after an evening at Maxim's.'

'You're exaggerating!'

'You think so? Let me tell you this. The management at L'Attentat are deeply concerned at last night's demonstration. They have asked me not to appear at the café for the next few nights until the public's feelings have abated. That, Inspector, is what you have achieved!'

Gautier began to grow annoyed at the injustice of what she was saying. 'Just pause to reflect, Mademoiselle. When I came to L'Attentat the other evening, I went to some trouble to conceal my identity, so that malicious people would not assume that you were under suspicion. I have told no one, not even my superiors, of the accusation that has been made against you. Count yourself fortunate. Another police officer might well have had you brought to Sûreté headquarters. He might even have made you appear before an examining magistrate.'

'On whose accusation?'

This time Gautier ignored her question. Instead he said: 'For two good reasons: firstly as you had been accused by someone close to the dead woman, secondly because you had lied to me.'

'That's absurd! How did I lie?'

'In saying that you did not know General Lafitte.'

Turning her head, she looked out of the window of the carriage. The lie must have been on her mind, if not on her conscience, for her to have realized at once to what Gautier was referring. It might also mean, Gautier reasoned, that perhaps this was the only lie she had told him.

'You don't know the circumstances of my relationship with the general,' she said at last.

'Then why not tell me?'

74

She turned to face him again and said bitterly: 'That was another of the humiliations which I suffered at the hands of Monterant. You know, I suppose, that General Lafitte was her lover?'

'I had heard so.'

'We met, the general and I, a few weeks ago. He seemed attracted to me and became very attentive, took me to dinner, sent me flowers and so on. We arranged to spend an evening together and I was certain he would declare his love for me. Instead, in the afternoon before we were going to meet, I received a box of chocolates from him.'

'With a diamond bracelet.'

'You've done your work well, Inspector. Yes, and a diamond bracelet, and with it a long letter saying that he loved another woman and had only been using me in the hope of making her jealous. Now he was ashamed of his behaviour and wished to apologize and the gift was his way of doing so.'

They were both silent. Gautier looked out of the window and saw that they had just passed Etoile and were travelling slowly down Avenue d'Iéna. He had supposed that they might be going to drive in the Bois de Boulogne which was the place where ladies rode in their carriages in the morning. Now he realized that she had probably given the coachman instructions to avoid the Bois in case they might be seen and recognized by any of her friends. That might also have been the reason why she had come that day not in the open Victoria which had met her at L'Attentat the previous evening, but in a closed Berline.

'Perhaps you understand now why I prefer to forget that I ever knew General Lafitte.'

'Yes, I do. But what I find less difficult to understand is why you should have attached so much importance to the friendship of a man more than twenty years older than you.'

He expected that she might be upset by the impertinence of the question, but she only shrugged her shoulders as she replied: 'As a man the general did not particularly interest me, but he has a position in Paris society. He is a regular and a welcome guest in all the best houses. He could have invited me to his own home and introduced me to the people who matter.'

'And does that mean so much to you? I would have thought you were rich enough and famous enough to have thumbed your nose to the gratin.'

'Only people who can never be accepted in society talk and think like that.'

Her attitude was beginning to irritate Gautier. He was not usually intolerant of human failings and could see why people who had nothing, the poor and the deprived, should envy those more fortunate than themselves. Clémentine Lyse's social aspirations and her jealousy of Sophie Monterant were to him inexcusable because she already had achieved so much. For an illegitimate child from the slums of Paris, to be successful, wealthy and popular with ordinary people should be enough.

'Did you say you would not be singing at L'Attentat tonight?' he asked her.

'That's right.'

'Then I wonder if you would do me the honour of accompanying me to a reception and musical evening.'

'Where?'

'At the home of the Comte and Comtesse de Limousin.'

'Is that supposed to be a joke?' She looked at him sharply. 'Or are you deliberately insulting me?'

'No, Mademoiselle. It's true that I have been invited to the comte's home. Look at this.'

From his pocket he pulled out the invitation card which the comtesse's secretary had given to him as he was leaving the house in Avenue du Bois the previous day. She had made it out to 'Monsieur J.-P. Gautier and Lady.' Clémentine took the card and read it through thoughtfully.

Eventually she said, with only a hint of bitterness: 'I was at a reception at the comtesse's house about a year ago. She was entertaining the King of the Belgians.'

'Really?'

'But not as guest. I was asked to go and sing for a very large fee. After I had sung they offered me refeshments—in the servants' hall, of course.'

Gautier took the card back. He was beginning to regret the slightly malicious impulse which had driven him to telling her about the comtesse's invitation. He said: 'In the circumstances I can hardly expect you to come with me to the reception. It was presumptuous of me to ask. I'm sorry.'

Unexpectedly she smiled. 'Don't apologize, Monsieur Gautier. I'm glad you invited me. And I shall be delighted to come as your partner.'

That evening Gautier did not have to steel himself against the feeling that usually engulfed him as he climbed three flights of stairs to an empty apartment; a feeling that was not so much loneliness as a sense of aimlessness and a reluctance to face the boredom of an evening with nothing to do. He was looking forward to the soirée at the home of the Comte de Limousin, not because he believed it was likely to be a pleasant social evening, nor for the pleasure of Clémentine Lyse's company. Social distractions had never held much appeal for him and he had the feeling that Clémentine Lyse, as a companion, might be at best self-assertive and demanding and at worst aggressive and difficult. What he hoped was that the evening might provide a challenge to his intelligence and information that might point him towards solving the riddle of Sophie Monterant's murder.

When he opened the door to his apartment, he found that the gas light in the small hallway was burning. He thought at first that the woman who cleaned for him must have forgotten to turn it off, but then realized that she came in the mornings when there was no need of light in the hallway. The knowledge that there was only one other possible explanation filled him with a momentary panic.

Fighting down a temptation to turn and leave, he went into the living-room and saw that his deduction was correct. Suzanne was sitting there waiting for him.

In the months that had passed since she had left him, Gautier had always assumed that one day she would come back. He had often imagined the meeting, anticipating what she would say, planning his response. Now, seeing her there, he wished she had not come. He had no desire to hear her apologize for her infidelity and ask him to take her back, not because he did not want her back, but because she would be forcing him into the rôle of forgiving husband. The feeling that it was he who should be forgiven

77

still persisted, an irritating sore that had never festered but also never healed.

'How are you, Jean-Paul?' she asked cautiously.

'Not too bad. And you?'

'You look thinner.'

The implication, he supposed, was that he had not been looked after properly. 'I needed to lose weight,' he said.

'I hope you don't mind my coming.'

'Of course not.'

He sat down in a chair opposite her. In some indefinable and scarcely perceptible way her appearance had changed. Shortly before she had left him, he remembered, he had observed that, although she was still not quite thirty, the first signs of approaching middle-age were already showing in her expression and in her mannerisms. She looked younger now, which might be the result of a new emotional experience, a burgeoning of passion.

'You have been so kind and so understanding already, Jean-Paul,' she said diffidently, 'that I scarcely know how to ask you this.'

He felt suddenly weary. 'What is it that you want?'

'When I left you, I told you I was not going to live with him.' Even after all these months she could not bring herself to name her lover.

'Yes. You did.'

'I came here tonight to ask you to release me from that promise.'

'Are you saying that you want to go and live with him?'

'Yes, I do.'

Gautier wanted to laugh, partly with relief and partly at his own conceit in assuming that she would wish to be with him again. He told her: 'You must do exactly as you wish, Suzanne. It's your life.'

'Thank you, Jean-Paul. As always you're too good to me. But it will be a great help to us. He's running a café now, you see, and it has living accommodation above it.'

'A café, eh?'

'Just a small place off Place Pigalle. My father set him up in it.'

78

Gautier felt a sharp stab of resentment. Suzanne's father and he had got on particularly well together and after she had left him he had missed the old man's companionship and his stories and the laughs they had shared. Morally it seemed wrong that his wife's lover should supplant him in his father-in-law's affections.

'So he's left the fifteenth arrondissement then?' Although he had not known the name of the man for whom Suzanne had left him, he had known that he was a policeman.

'Oh yes. Some time ago.'

'You were wise to persuade him to try another métier. Life in the police is hard on a marriage.'

'He didn't leave the police on my account. He did it for your sake.'

'Mine?'

'He thought it would make things difficult for you if your colleagues knew.'

'Knew what? That I'd been made a cuckold by another policeman?' Suzanne looked hurt and, regretting his words, he at once wanted to make up for them. He said: 'I'm happy for you, Suzanne, really I am. And I hope the café's a success.'

She rose to leave. He could see that there was something more she wished to say. Finally she said: 'Would you be willing to meet him sometime, Jean-Paul? I'd like you to.'

He knew then that this was to be his act of atonement. So he smiled and said: 'If that will please you.'

'You will? You promise?'

'Of course.'

'Then come to the café any evening.' She put a hand on his arm. 'And come soon.'

10

WHEN CLÉMENTINE LYSE's carriage drew to a halt outside the home of the Comtesse de Limousin, a footman in green and silver livery came forward to open the carriage door so that she and Gautier could dismount. A crowd of onlookers had gathered in Avenue du Bois to watch the guests arrive, to admire the brilliance of the carriages, the beauty of the women's gowns, the dignity of the men in full evening dress. This could only mean that the soirée was to be a spectacular event attended by distinguished people. Parisians had a fine sense of occasion and would never turn out to watch the second-rate or the commonplace.

Another footman stood outside the entrance to the house, one more at the foot of the broad staircase and yet another at the top. Gautier's evening cloak, top hat and gloves were unobtrusively taken from him and he and his partner climbed the stairs to the first floor.

A major-domo standing at the entrance to the drawing-room took his invitation and called out their names. 'Monsieur Jean-Paul Gautier and Mademoiselle Lyse.'

Some eighty or ninety people were assembled in the drawing-room, standing in small groups or in pairs and talking. A few of them glanced towards the door, mildly curious, as the names were called out but most of them were too immersed in their own conversations to show any interest in new arrivals. Gautier supposed that Clémentine would take this as a slight, accustomed as she must be to public acclaim.

The Comte and Comtesse de Limousin were stationed just inside the door to receive their guests. The comte nodded his head in a bow while the comtesse allowed Gautier to raise her hand to his lips.

She said: 'My husband and I are delighted you could come, Monsieur. Please go and join the other guests. The music will be starting shortly.'

Gautier and Clémentine moved into the room and took the tall, fluted glasses of champagne which a manservant offered them. The people gathered in the vast drawing-room provided a brilliant spectacle. All the men were wearing full evening dress while the long evening gowns of the ladies were mostly in white or pale colours but decorated with bows or ribbons or flowers in bright, contrasting crimsons or blues or gold. Some wore tiaras, some had flowers in their hair, and diamonds, sapphires and rubies sparkled in a contest of opulence.

Clémentine looked as attractive as any woman in the room. She was wearing a pale yellow dress, decorated with blue silk at the neckline and sleeves, with a line of small blue bows running down to the waist and a large blue bow on one side of the full, gathered skirt. Her neck and shoulders were bare except for a diamond and sapphire necklace which matched a pair of flower-shaped ear-rings. Like all of the women in the room she wore long white gloves and like many of them she carried a fan, for fans were in vogue at the time, useful it was said not only to provide a cool draught in overheated rooms but, when folded, to admonish the straying fingers of over-bold admirers.

A platform had been erected at the far end of the room with a grand piano in place on it and about fifty gilt chairs had been arranged in rows to face it. The chairs were for the ladies, Gautier realized, and all but the elderly and infirm among the men would be expected to stand. Gloomily he wondered how long the brilliant young pianist's performance was likely to last.

'The comte and comtesse have an impressive circle of friends,' Clémentine remarked. 'All Paris is here.'

'Who, for instance?'

'There's the Prince de Wagram for one. He's that small wizened man by the fireplace. The couple to whom he's talking are the banker Nathaniel Granz and his wife. There, look, that woman taking a glass of champagne from the footman is the new Princesse de Volnay. She's the daughter of the American railroad millionaire, Jay Leacock.'

81

'You're very well informed!'

Clémentine nodded towards the entrance where a short man with white hair accompanied by a slim, dark-haired woman who had just arrived were being received by the comte and comtesse. 'That couple is the Minister of Beaux-arts and his wife.'

'Is that the man whom you described as an ageing lecher?' Gautier asked.

'Good Heavens, no! I was talking of the man who was minister when I entered the Conservatoire ten years ago. This one is Henri Charvet.'

Gautier remembered that he had seen the name in Sophie Monterant's address book. 'Do you know him?'

A shadow of discontent passed across Clémentine's face as she replied: 'I was presented to him once at a charity concert. He goes to the theatre, concerts and art salons regularly, but I suppose he would hardly consider singing at a caf'conc' as art.'

While she was speaking, Gautier noticed that the Comtesse de Limousin had mounted the platform at the end of the room. She was accompanied by a young man with longish hair and an expression which some might have thought soulful but which anyone who had moved among the poor of Paris might be forgiven for believing to be the result of prolonged under-nourishment.

'My friends,' the comtesse said to her guests, 'it is my great pleasure to present to you this evening a brilliant young pianist, Monsieur Roger Delorme.'

The audience clapped, Monsieur Delorme stepped forward and bowed, and the comtesse continued: 'Monsieur Delorme will play for us a programme of contemporary music: three songs by Claude Debussy and a piano concerto by a foreign composer who has made his home not far from here at Fontainebleau, Frederick Delius. So could I ask you now to take your seats.'

Some of the ladies had already found themselves seats and the rest now moved forward to take up the remainder of the gilt chairs. The men stood at the back, some of them placing themselves by the mantelpiece of the fireplace or near the walls, where they could surreptitiously get a little support during the recital. Most of them, though, had stoically endured the discomfort of standing through a concert many times before.

The pianist sat down and began to play Debussy's setting of a poem by Verlaine. He had played no more than the opening bars when Gautier felt someone touch his elbow from behind. Looking round he saw one of the footmen, who whispered to him: 'Monsieur le Comte wishes to speak with you in the study, Monsieur Gautier.'

He followed the man out of the drawing-room and downstairs to a room at the back of the house. It was a large room, lined on one wall with bookshelves, while the others were decorated with trophies of the chase. The comte was sitting at a desk smoking a cigar, looking completely at ease and probably thankful to have escaped the piano recital.

'I understand that you wish to see me, Inspector Gautier.' In spite of his relaxed air, the comte sounded displeased.

'Yes, sir.'

'I find it most irregular. If the Sûreté wished to ask me for information, the director should have made an appointment.' Gautier made no comment and the comte went on: 'However, to please my wife, who arranged this little charade, I agreed to see you, but not in front of the guests.'

'I am obliged to you, Monsieur le Comte.'

The comte was slim in build and had fair hair and an exquisitely cultivated fair moustache. His pink complexion and long eyelashes might have looked effeminate, had it not been for his hard, blue eyes. Gautier, who did not as a rule make premature judgements of people, decided instinctively that Comte Edmond de Limousin was not only proud, vain and arrogant, but intelligent enough to be a dangerous adversary.

'The comtesse says that you're making enquiries into the death of Madame Sophie Monterant.'

'That's correct.'

'I cannot imagine why you should suppose that I can help you.'

'We are speaking to all her friends in the hope that they might know of some reason why Madame Monterant was poisoned and of someone who might have poisoned her.'

'What makes you believe I was a friend of hers?'

The comte had not suggested that Gautier should sit down in the empty chair on the other side of his desk. Clearly this was going

83

to be another interview in the Limousin home when Gautier would be expected to remain standing like a servant. It was irritation more than anything which made him decide to stretch the truth in what he said next.

'Madame Monterant left papers to show that you provided part of the finances for her most recent production. She also left a diary.'

The comte had been taught in his upbringing not to show his feelings, particularly before people of inferior rank, and it was only a momentary hesitation which betrayed that he was disconcerted. He told Gautier: 'There's no point in denying that I had seen a good deal of Madame Monterant over the past few years. My wife has probably told you that. She finds a perverse delight in boasting of my infidelities, just to prove how modern and broadminded she is.'

'In that case you may know whether Madame Monterant had any enemies.'

'A good many, I imagine. She was a woman who inspired envy.'

'People don't usually kill for envy.'

'Surely, Inspector, you must have some thoughts on who might have sent the poisoned chocolates?'

'Only one name has been seriously suggested as a possible assassin.'

'And what name is that?'

'The singer Clémentine Lyse.'

'Isn't that the woman who is with you tonight?'

'Yes.'

The comte laughed, but without humour. One felt that he seldom allowed himself the luxury of humour. 'That presumably means you don't believe she was responsible.'

'Frankly, no.'

'Has it occurred to you, Inspector, that it might have been someone much closer to Sophie?'

'Do you mean one of her relatives?'

'No. I had in mind her maid, Françoise.'

Gautier made no attempt to conceal his surprise. He said: 'But the woman was devoted to her mistress.'

'You might have formed that impression, but I can assure you

84

that recently Sophie was far from satisfied with the maid's behaviour. She had occasion to rebuke her more than once and very severely. Françoise, it seemed, was getting above herself and interfering in her mistress's private life.'

'I doubt if a rebuke, however severe, would be sufficient motive for killing her mistress.'

The comte shook his head to express his doubt. 'Don't be too certain, Inspector. Françoise came from the country, a village near Grasse, I believe. You don't know country people as well as I do.'

Gautier refrained from telling him that he had been born and brought up in the country. The comte went on: 'Country people are closer to nature than you and I; more elemental if you like. Killing another human being is no more to them than wringing a chicken's neck. And have you made any enquiries to find out whether Françoise stood to gain by her mistress's death? I should be very surprised if Sophie had not made provision for her servant in her will.'

After the recital was over the comte and comtesse circulated among their guests. The chairs were quickly taken from the room, more champagne brought in and the guests, freed of the distraction of music, were able to engage in the more serious business of conversation.

To his surprise, Gautier met someone he knew, Maître Bonnard, one of the most fashionable and successful lawyers in France, whom he had met more than once in the Palais de Justice during criminal cases. He introduced Clémentine to the lawyer and his wife.

'Surely we've met before,' Madame Bonnard said to Clémentine.

'I don't think so, Madame.'

It struck Gautier that Bonnard and his wife might well have heard Clémentine sing at L'Attentat or one of the other small caf'conc's patronized by society and the wealthy bourgeoisie, but now failed to recognize her. Off stage and particularly in evening dress, Clémentine looked quite unlike the character whom she portrayed when she sang. He wondered whether a woman who set such store by success might not feel disappointed or even slighted when people did not recognize either her face or her name.

As they were talking to the Bonnards, the Comte and Comtesse

85

de Limousin approached. The comtesse said: 'I'm going to take you away from your friends, Monsieur Gautier. There is someone here who particularly wishes to meet you.' She turned to her husband and added: 'You'll look after Mademoiselle Lyse, won't you Edmond?'

She led Gautier away from the group and across the room to where the Minister of Beaux-arts was talking to a very plain woman with straight hair and a fat man with a face of a mournful dog.

'The minister, Henri Charvet, has heard that you're investigating the death of Sophie Monterant. He particularly asked for you to be presented to him.'

'Who told him, I wonder,' Gautier remarked, 'about my official duties?'

The comtesse smiled and shrugged her shoulders. 'My husband, in all probability.'

When they reached the minister, she extricated him from the people to whom he was talking with the same dexterity as she had separated Gautier from Clémentine and the Bonnards. Then, after making the introductions, she left them together. Although short in stature, the minister was an imposing man, mainly on account of his large, handsome head and abundant, white hair and bushy eyebrows. It was the head of a talented and forceful man, Gautier thought, more suited to a great composer than a politician.

'I felt I had to ask you,' Charvet said, 'what progress you've made in establishing who might have killed Madame Monterant.'

'Very little, I'm afraid, Monsieur le Ministre.'

'One can understand that. It must be difficult even to find anyone who would have wished to kill her.'

'You knew her then?'

'One of the most brilliant, even the most brilliant of our younger actresses? I would have been failing in my duty as minister if I had not known her. I had seen her act several times. Did you ever see her Phèdre, Monsieur Gautier?'

'Unfortunately, no.'

'Then you missed a great theatrical experience. Many good judges thought that her interpretation of Phèdre was better than Bernhardt's and as good as Réjane's. Do you know the speech in the second act when Phèdre tells Hippolyte she loves him? I have never heard it delivered with such passion and such sensitivity. One could see the anguish on Sophie's face, torn as the queen is between a love which is stronger than she is and a guilty revulsion for a passion which she knows to be forbidden.'

It seemed to Gautier that he was listening to a well-rehearsed speech, designed to convince an audience that not only the actress but the Minister of Beaux-arts himself was a person of sensitivity and understanding.

Charvet continued: 'My predecessors and I can justly be proud of the encouragement which we have given to this brilliant actress.'

'And yet she walked out of the Comédie-Française. Didn't you feel that was a betrayal?'

'It didn't happen during my ministry,' Charvet said primly, implying that such a distasteful event could never have occurred in his. 'As a matter of fact, Inspector, I had been trying for some time to persuade Madame Monterant to rejoin our national theatre. And I have reason to believe that she might have agreed.'

'That would have meant a great financial sacrifice on her part.'

'Admittedly, but she might have done it for France. Do you realize, Monsieur, that our country is today the centre of the world in art, culture and fashion? Paris is a magnet for writers, painters, musicians and poets from all over the world. They flock here from England, from America, Spain, Italy, Russia, because here they find not only freedom, but inspiration. All this has happened in our lifetime, since the last war. From the ashes of that defeat a new phoenix has arisen, a new France.'

Gautier decided it was time he reminded the minister that they were supposed to be discussing Sophie Monterant. He said: 'Did you ever visit Madame Monterant's home, Minister?'

Charvet seemed surprised at the question. 'Me? Yes, more than once. We were good friends.' He gave Gautier what must have been intended as a boyish smile. 'Mind you, I would have been delighted to have been more than just Sophie's friend. But, poor girl, she was almost exactly half my age. It's terribly sad, isn't it? She might have gone on thrilling us with her acting for another thirty years. Why not? Bernhardt's as good as ever.'

'They say Monterant put on *La Dame aux Camélias* at the

Châtelet just to defy Bernhardt, who's appearing at her own theatre just across the road.'

'Yes, I believe she did. It was just a piece of youthful bravado. She could never have knocked Sarah from her pedestal. And talking of Sarah reminds me that she had promised to appear in a charity matinée which my wife is organizing in aid of the victims of that earthquake in Algeria. Would you like to attend, Monsieur Gautier? You seem interested in the theatre.'

'I would be very pleased to support it, Minister,' Gautier replied, wondering how much tickets at a charity matinée would cost and whether Courtrand could be persuaded that the Sûreté should pay.

'No, no, you'll come as our guest, of course.' Charvet looked across the room. 'Ah, there is Madame Charvet. I'll call her over.'

The minister's wife was talking to a small group of other guests, but when she saw her husband beckon she came over. Gautier saw that she was quite clearly a good deal younger than Charvet, probably in her mid-forties. She had a pretty face, with dark eyes and delicate features, which was only partly spoilt by a petulant mouth and a weak, receding chin.

'Inspector Gautier will be coming to the Sarah Bernhardt matinée as our guest, Adèle. Would you arrange for him to be sent two tickets?'

'All right.' Madame Charvet seemed irritated by her husband's peremptory tone, but although her expression was far from cordial, the look she gave Gautier was not without interest. He had seen the same look on the faces of other women, but not of women in society. Madame Charvet, to use a popular expression of the day, had eyes that were not at all cold.

'We live in Rue de Grenelle, Monsieur,' she said to Gautier. 'Do you ever pass by there in the course of duty? If so, perhaps you could call at the house and pick up the tickets.'

'My dear!' the minister protested. 'Monsieur Gautier doesn't patrol the streets. He's a senior inspector at the Sûreté and something of a celebrity.'

'I would be delighted to call, Madame,' Gautier said, 'at any time to suit your convenience.'

'Good. Come in the morning. I'm usually at home then.'

*   *   *

As they were being driven home from Avenue du Bois, Clémentine seemed, for the first time since Gautier had met her, relaxed and contented. She talked with pleasure of the evening and of the people they had met and appeared to have forgotten her obsession with Sophie Monterant. Listening to her, Gautier was reminded of a child returning home from a visit to the theatre, with the excitement of unreality still holding her imagination captive.

The Comte de Limousin, she told him, had been attentive and kind and had presented her to any number of his friends. She named them to Gautier in succession, explaining what position they held in society and, in the case of women, what they had been wearing and anything amusing or witty that had been said to her.

'And the Minister of Beaux-arts,' she said to Gautier, 'what was he like?'

'Indestructibly charming.'

'What did you two talk about?'

'He delivered a political speech and I listened well; so well that he rewarded me with two tickets to a charity matinée.'

When her carriage stopped in Rue de Courcelles and he alighted to hold the door open for her, Clémentine said: 'Why don't you come up for a few minutes? My maid will prepare us some refreshment.'

'Isn't it rather late? You must be tired.'

'Me? Not at all. We're all night birds in the theatre.'

It could only be an actress or courtesan, Gautier thought, who would invite him to her apartment at that time of night. Although convention was being rapidly eroded and ladies of modern views were claiming more liberty, no respectable single woman would have even accompanied him unchaperoned to the comtesse's soirée, much less taken him back to her home.

A sleepy concierge let them into the building and a pretty maid of about seventeen opened the door of Clémentine's apartment to them. It was on the first floor and more spacious than Sophie Monterant's home in nearby Rue Murillo. Gautier wondered whether it was only by coincidence that she was living so close to the dead actress.

89

The apartment was also more tastefully furnished than Monterant's. The furniture was without exception of the highest quality, the carpets and curtains blended well to give an impression of ease and comfort. Like every other society or bourgeois drawing-room it was full of ornaments and bric-à-brac, but these too had been tastefully chosen and arranged. The only thing connected with her professional life that Gautier could see was the original design for a poster advertising her appearance at the Divan Japonais. It had been executed in a style made famous by Toulouse-Lautrec, in simple flowing lines that made it almost a caricature.

'Bring me a tisane,' Clémentine told the maid and then turning to Gautier she asked him: 'What will you have? Cognac?'

'Cognac will be fine.'

The maid left the room taking her mistress's cloak and Gautier's hat and gloves. Clémentine sat down on a sofa and made a gesture to show that Gautier should join her.

'Did you enjoy this evening?' she asked him.

'Very much.'

'But you hadn't expected to, had you?'

'To be honest, no. I haven't the disposition for social functions, and as far as art is concerned, I'm a philistine.'

'Then why did you enjoy it?'

'Because it appeared to give you pleasure.'

'I believe you mean that.'

'I do.' Although his answer had sounded like a shallow compliment, Gautier realized to his surprise that he had meant it.

The maid brought in the tisane, an infusion of herbs popular at the time with ladies much concerned with their waistlines. With it on a silver tray was a decanter of cognac and a glass. She gave her mistress the tisane, poured the cognac for Gautier and set the tray down on a table. Clémentine told her that she would not be needed any further and she could go to bed.

After she had left the room Gautier said: 'She's very good-looking, that girl.'

'Marie-France? Yes. Single women like myself, actresses and courtesans, can get maids without any difficulty. Pretty young girls with ambition are always looking for positions in the house of an attractive mistress with lots of admirers. They know there will be opportunities for them to arouse the interest of men who visit the house, and, if they are clever, in no time at all they can be set up by a rich admirer in an apartment of their own.'

'In other words they pick up the crumbs from the mistress's table?'

'One could put it like that.'

'Is Marie-France available, do you know?' Gautier intended the question as a joke.

'I'm sure she is, but a guest at the table doesn't need to bend down and pick up crumbs.'

Clémentine smiled at him as she spoke. At any other time and with any other woman Gautier would have taken the remark for an invitation, but until that moment Clémentine had said or done nothing to suggest that she would have welcomed any attentions from him. So he sipped his cognac and made no comment.

'Are you married, Jean-Paul?' It was the first time she had used his Christian name.

'Yes, but my wife left me some months ago for another man.'

'Did you mind very much?'

'Not as much as I should have, I suppose.'

'What does that mean?'

'The greatest insult to a Frenchman's vanity is to be made a cuckold.'

'You're not a vain man,' Clémentine remarked, 'but I suspect that your wife's unfaithfulness has hurt more than your pride.'

'I bear her no ill-will.'

'Possibly not, but if she has not hurt you, why are you so reserved and unapproachable, so mistrustful of women?'

'Am I?' Gautier felt that he should have resented her questions, coming as they did from a woman who scarcely knew him, but he did not.

'Yes. Either that or you're being unbelievably obtuse.' She laid a hand on his arm. 'Or is it that you find me so unattractive?'

This time there could be no mistaking the invitation. As he kissed her, Gautier found to his surprise that she did attract him. The first impression he had formed of her when seeing her on stage and in their early conversations, an image of a woman self-centred and cold, had distorted his perception. Now in the softness of her lips and their responses to his own, he could sense a tenderness and a passion that was wholly unexpected.

After the first kiss she sighed and lay back in his arms. His glance fell on her throat, bare shoulders and the curve of her breasts barely concealed by the décolletage of her dress and he felt desire mounting inside him. He kissed her again and this time her lips parted. Placing her hands on the back of his neck, she drew him to her fiercely, her fingers entwining themselves in his hair. When he stroked her neck and shoulders, she gasped and started to tremble.

He withdrew his mouth from hers to regain his breath and she looked at him with troubled eyes, but before he could speak she kissed him again and slipping her hands under his coat began drawing her finger-nails down his spine. He felt his self-control slipping.

'Shouldn't we go to your bedroom?'

She turned her face abruptly away from his and lay in his arms, passively, without speaking. For perhaps a minute she did not move and he sensed that she was fighting some inner battle. Then he felt her body stiffen. She pushed him away from her and leapt to her feet.

'How dare you!' The fury in her voice, because it was unexpected, sounded unreal. 'Do you imagine that I'm a whore or some little dressmaker who would be flattered to allow a policeman into her bed?'

'I'm sorry,' he began.

'Sorry?' She put a cutting edge of sarcasm on her words. 'Next you'll be saying it's an accident, a case of mistaken identity.'

'Why did you ask me back here tonight?'

'You may well ask. To show my gratitude, I suppose. Because you had invited me out, given me an evening which I enjoyed and which may prove useful to my career.'

'Is that all?'

'Isn't that enough?' she countered, misinterpreting his question. 'How much do you expect for a couple of glasses of champagne and an indifferent piano recital?'

'So you dispense your favours in proportion to the value of what you receive?'

'If you like to put it that way, why not?'

Her voice was hard, her expression scornful. Gautier stood up, still not able to believe that she meant what she was saying and unwilling to accept that the passion she had begun to show only a few minutes earlier had been suddenly frozen within her.

He told her: 'Well, if what you did just now was just a display of gratitude, you must be a fine actress.'

She laughed. 'So you do believe that I wanted to give myself to a policeman?'

'No,' Gautier could not resist the impulse to strike back. 'I suppose it would have to be an impresario or a theatre manager, someone who could give you a fat contract.'

She called him an obscene name. It was an epithet he had often heard used in the meat market and sleazy cafés and by soldiers hanging around outside their barracks, but seldom in the elegant apartments of Plaine Monceau.

'Mademoiselle,' he replied politely, 'you have made your feelings more than clear. There is no point in prolonging our evening together. Goodnight.'

11

THE REPORTS OF three inspectors who had carried out the enquiries Courtrand had ordered in connection with the Pelotti affair were circulated to all those concerned. Next morning in his office Gautier read them.

It had been quickly established that in the interval between the killing of Lucie Bertron and his arrest, Pelotti had not been hiding in the underworld, but had lived under the name of Georges Auguste in the Hôtel de la Reine. Once again Gautier was amazed by the man's audacity. The hotel was a small but stylish establishment in Rue de Rivoli, within easy walking distance of Sûreté headquarters.

The jewellery belonging to Lucie Bertron had also been traced. All the pieces had been sold to a respectable jeweller in Avenue de l'Opéra by a Monsieur Georges Auguste, who had explained that they belonged to his niece. The story he had given was that his niece had been abandoned by her husband in precarious financial circumstances and he had produced a letter from her authorizing Monsieur Auguste to sell the jewellery at the best price he could get. The jeweller had been shown a photograph of Pelotti and had identified him as the man who had posed as Monsieur Auguste.

Gautier was surprised to see that the sale of the jewellery had realized only 20,000 francs. The pearl necklace, supposed to be worth 200,000, had proved to be almost worthless, a copy of the kind that ladies often had made as a protection against the original being stolen. Further enquiries had revealed that Lucie Bertron had sold her original necklace more than five years previously, well before she had even met Pelotti and invested the money in American railroad stock.

Attached to the inspectors' reports was a brief note from the director, stating that he was now satisfied he had sufficient evidence to show without any doubt that Pelotti had killed Lucie Bertron and that robbery was his motive. No further enquiries would be made unless these were ordered by the juge d'instruction at a later stage.

And that, Gautier thought, is the end of Marcel Pelotti.

Gautier had just finished reading when Surat came in to report on the work he had been doing in the Monterant affair. He first placed on his chief's desk a list which the chocolatiers had prepared of all the people and addresses to whom their spring boxes of chocolates had been delivered. The list, neatly hand-written, ran into several pages and Gautier flicked through it.

'Labiche do good business,' he remarked.

'Yes. I'm afraid the list is too long to be of any practical value. There could be no possible way of tracing all those boxes. Most of them will have been destroyed long ago.'

'I agree. Have you read right through it?'

'Yes, Patron.'

'Did you find any names which might be connected with the Monterant affair?'

'Some, but that's not surprising as almost all of the rich or desirable women in Paris appear to have been sent a box. The Comtesse de Limousin received one.'

'Do you recall if one was sent to the wife of the Minister of Beaux-arts, Madame Adèle Charvet?'

'It so happens that I do. She received no less than three.'

Gautier placed the list on his desk again. 'As you say, we won't get much out of this but I'll study it later.'

'There's one more thing,' Surat said. 'I know it has no bearing on the death of Monterant, but Lucie Bertron was sent a box as well.'

'Do you know who sent it?'

'Yes. A young lieutenant in the Hussars.'

'Chocolates were probably all the poor chap could afford,' Gautier remarked drily. 'Army pay would never rise to a night with Lucie.'

Next Surat told him of the enquiries he had made at the Châtelet theatre. These had been totally unrewarding. No one in the theatre or associated with Sophie Monterant's production of *La Dame aux Camélias* would seem to have had the slightest motive for wishing her dead. On the contrary, most of them had been to a greater or lesser extent dependent on her or at least on the success of the production.

'She wasn't liked,' Surat explained, 'for she was high-handed and had an inflated idea of her own ability. At the same time everyone concedes that, however hard she worked them, she was scrupulously fair and never went back on her word. That counts for a lot in the theatre.'

'Did she have anyone understudying her part?'

'Someone who might look for a brief moment of glory? No. Without Sophie the play would have been nothing. As you probably know the production was suspended the day after her death and it won't be restarted.'

'It's a strange thing!' Gautier remarked. 'Monterant was a woman whom several men loved, whom nobody liked and who appears to have been wholly without sympathy, pity or charity, and yet we can't find anyone who might have hated her enough to have killed her.'

'Except Clémentine Lyse.'

'As you say, except for Mademoiselle Lyse. We must keep looking, but let's try another approach. Monterant must have been a wealthy woman. Find out the name of her banker. Go to see him and then if necessary try her lawyer. There may well be someone who stood to gain financially from her death.'

After Surat had left, Gautier unlocked his desk drawer and took out the leather-bound books which had belonged to Sophie Monterant. It was the diary that interested him most and he re-read some of the entries that had caught his eye when he had first glanced through it.

Now that he knew more of the actress's background, he was sure he would be able to identify at least two of the men to whom she had referred in the diary by code names. Her most recent lover, 'Rimrod', who had backed her play with his wife's money, could only be the Comte de Limousin, while the jealous 'Monge', whom he had supplanted, would be General Lafitte.

The other names—'Labiste', 'Jockey' and 'Spumantisi'—were more difficult to match with anyone whom he had met or heard about. 'Spumantisi', he thought, could conceivably be the Minister of Beaux-arts. Gautier looked again at the entry in the diary where the name occurred. '. . . Had a petit bleu from Spumantisi in the afternoon wishing me luck for tomorrow. I hope he keeps his promise to attend. It would lend quite a cachet to the first performance.'

To have the Minister of Beaux-arts present at the first performance would certainly give distinction to any production. He looked back through the preceding pages of the diary, but could find no other reference to Spumantisi. He did, however, come across one other name which might equally well have referred to the minister. Back in February, there was the following entry: 'Brainemist is being very attentive all of a sudden. Today he talked to me for a long time at the Charity Bazaar and paid me fulsome compliments. He hinted that his friendship could be helpful to my career, which of course is true. Am I too young, do you suppose, for the Légion d'Honneur?'

The attentive 'Brainemist' had also visited Sophie in her apartment, where not everyone had welcomed him. The maid, Françoise, appeared to have taken an instant dislike to him. 'Brainemist called in the morning. I kept him waiting while I finished dressing and during that time Françoise must have been very rude to him and when I arrived he was quite upset. I hope the silly woman has not put him off coming again.'

Seeing the name of Françoise in the diary reminded Gautier of the suggestion which the Comte de Limousin had made that she might have been responsible for Monterant's death. He glanced through the diary to see if there were any other entries which might show an enmity between mistress and maid and found one towards the end of April which read:

Françoise left today to spend a few days with her family in Grasse, laden not only with a bulging valise but with bags full of parcels which can only have contained provisions. She must have had enough there to keep her family for a month or more. When I asked her what she was taking, she said it was only the cakes and fruit and sweets which had been presents to me and which I had passed over to her. She claimed she had been saving them up, which I find impossible to believe, knowing how greedy she is. She can never resist gobbling up anything tasty and sweet. I am sure she has been taking food surreptitiously out of what she buys for the house, probably in collusion with the tradesmen and keeping it to take home. When I suggested as much, we had a fine scene! Indignant denials, followed by oaths on the Blessed Virgin, followed by tears. However she did not offer to let me search her baggage and in a weak moment I did not insist. The lesson to be learned is that I must scrutinize the household accounts more carefully. These peasants are all thieves.

Although the incident gave an insight into the character of Sophie Monterant, Gautier could see nothing in it to suggest that Françoise might have hated her mistress enough to wish to kill her. The only other recent reference to the maid's behaviour came a day or two later. 'Brainemist has, I suspect, been avoiding Françoise since their quarrel. Taking advantage of her absence in the country, I invited him home for an intimate souper à deux. He has been good to me and deserved a reward, but what a fiasco the evening turned out to be!'

Gautier decided that even now the diary was going to tell him little of consequence about Sophie Monterant's love affairs and certainly not enough for him to know whether the Minister of Beaux-arts might have been one of them. On the other hand he might learn more from the minister's wife and he did have a reason for calling on her. Rue de Grenelle was only a short walk away on the Left Bank. He locked the diary away once more, relieved to have an excuse for leaving the office.

On his way downstairs he met Lemaire, the inspector who had originally been sent by the Sûreté to Sophie Monterant's apartment on the night of her death and who had persuaded Gautier to take over the investigation from him. Lemaire was coming out of the director's office and they walked down to the ground floor together.

'How is your wife?' Gautier asked.

'Physically in good health, but very fretful. The baby still hasn't arrived.'

'The waiting is the worst part, everyone says.'

'And how are you progressing in the Monterant affair?' Lemaire asked.

'Up to the present I haven't any idea of who might have killed her.'

'I'm sorry I let you in for such a difficult investigation.'

'Don't apologize. I'm enjoying it really. For the first time in my life I'm learning how the upper crust lives.'

'I've just been given a soft job. Courtrand wants me to help him on the Pelotti affair.'

'Really? I thought I was supposed to be doing that.'

'He asked me to tell you he won't need you any more. There's nothing much to be done anyway. He has enough evidence to send Pelotti to the guillotine. My duties will simply be to escort him from prison to the office of the juge d'instruction every morning and take him back afterwards. It will mean I'll be home early every evening, which will please my wife.'

'Good for you! And I hope all goes well with your wife.'

As he crossed the Seine by Pont Saint-Michel, Gautier found himself thinking yet again of the scene at Clémentine's apartment the previous night. The memory of the humiliation still lingered, unwanted, in his mind. He had argued to himself that it was she who had been at fault, deliberately provoking his desire and then scornfully rejecting him, either through mere caprice or for the pleasure of wanton cruelty. Try as he might to exorcise the memory, it still returned, troubling him as an unsightly scar never ceases to trouble a sensitive woman. He had toyed with the idea of revenge but that, he knew, would only have been proof of his own weakness.

The Minister of Beaux-arts lived in an attractive but surprisingly unpretentious house in Rue de Grenelle. Gautier noticed a policeman standing unostentatiously not far from the entrance to the building. Ever since the President of France, Sadi Carnot, had been assassinated a few years previously, the police had been keeping a watchful eye on the houses of government ministers.

A maid opened the door of the Charvets' house to him and he

explained that he had called to collect the tickets which the minister had promised him for the charity matinée. She went to speak to her mistress and when she returned, told him that Madame would be happy to see him. He followed her to the drawing-room, where Madame Charvet was waiting.

'Inspector Gautier, I'm delighted to see you again so soon. Come and sit down.'

He went and joined her on the straight-backed Louis XV sofa on which she was sitting. As he did so he recalled the similar invitation which had been made to him not long ago by Clémentine Lyse.

'That was a very pretty girl you were escorting last night,' Madame Charvet remarked.

'Yes. She's Clémentine Lyse, the singer.'

'Really? I had assumed she was your wife.'

'My wife and I are separated, Madame.'

'I'm sorry. That was tactless of me.'

'There is no need to apologize. She left me for another man and probably she was right to do so. In any case I bear her no ill-will.'

'You surprise me.' The news that Gautier had been cuckolded appeared to arouse neither Madame Charvet's sympathy nor her disapproval, but only her curiosity. 'It's rare for a Frenchwoman to leave her husband. Though sometimes we take our revenge in other ways.'

'Revenge? For what?'

'The way you men treat us. Do you know that when a girl friend of mine went on honeymoon to Switzerland, her husband's mistress travelled by the same train in another compartment and he had taken a room for the creature in the same hotel. And that's by no means unusual. Men have mistresses before they are married and usually soon afterwards. It's not considered immoral. In fact many people look askance at a man who doesn't have a mistress. Women are not allowed the same freedom by society.'

'That's true.' Gautier had to concede that she was right.

'And so we take our revenge on men. We too have our love affairs.' She turned her head so that she was looking straight into Gautier's eyes. 'Do you blame us?'

'Not if you put it like that.'

'Then you're an understanding man; like my husband.'

Gautier made no comment. The Minister of Beaux-arts had not struck him as a man of liberal or modern ideas. Even so he had no reason to disbelieve Madame Charvet. He only wondered why she had chosen to tell him this.

She continued: 'Of course, the minister is aware that I'm much younger than him and that may be part of the reason why he allows me so much freedom. I repay him by being discreet. His political ambitions mean so much to Henri and I would never do anything that might damage his career.'

'The minister is well respected.' Gautier knew nothing of Charvet's reputation or ministerial ability but he hoped that his remark might end a conversation which was becoming tortuous, if not pointless, and might well end by being embarrassing.

Madame Charvet may have sensed his unease, for she stood up and said: 'I'll go and fetch your tickets, Monsieur Gautier. They should be in Henri's study.'

Gautier rose as she did and while she was out of the room, he went to look at a painting, which was hanging opposite the door. It was a landscape, a view of distant hills covered in mimosa which sloped down to a distant sea-shore fringed with palm trees. The artist, using a technique that was unfamiliar to Gautier, with the paint applied in thick splodges of bold colour, had created a wonderful impression of brilliant light on a hot, airless, summer's day. While he was still looking at the painting, Madame Charvet returned and joined him.

'Do you like it?' she asked.

'Very much.'

'It was painted by a very good friend of ours in the South. The minister comes from that part of the world and we still have a house there. His family had a very successful perfume business.'

She had been standing next to Gautier as they looked at the painting and as she turned away to return to the centre of the room, he felt her breasts brush against his arm. It might have been accidental, but he did not think so. He had known other women use that device to remind men that they were desirable and not inaccessible. Adèle Charvet, he noticed, although small and slim, had a body that was both well-made and well preserved.

She said: 'I'm sorry, Inspector, we must have given away all the tickets which we had in the house for the matinée. I'll ask my husband to bring some more home from the ministry. Would it inconvenience you to call again another day?'

'Not at all, Madame.'

'That will be nice. I'll telephone you at the Sûreté in a day or two to let you know when I'll be at home.'

'Thank you.'

She tugged at a bell-pull to call the maid, presumably to show Gautier out. 'The minister thinks very highly of you, Monsieur Gautier,' she said. 'And so do I. Our friendship could be very helpful to you, especially if we move across the river.'

'Across the river?'

'There, I'm being indiscreet again. Still, it isn't a secret any more. As you know the president is due to retire in a few weeks' time. Henri's name is among those from whom his successor will be chosen.'

The maid came into the room and stood by the door. As she held her hand out to him, Madame Charvet smiled. He bent forward to kiss her hand and as he did so she suddenly twisted her wrist, offering him not the back of the hand but the palm, slightly cupped.

Gautier was disconcerted, not knowing what was expected of him and merely brushed it with his lips. The perfume she was wearing on her wrists had a very distinctive aroma, delicate and dry almost to the point of bitterness.

She said softly: 'Your wife's lover, Monsieur Gautier, must have been a very attractive man.'

12

'MONSIEUR?'

The waiter at the Café Corneille looked at Gautier, awaiting his order. Gautier, uncertain of what he wanted as an apéritif, looked at Duthrey's glass.

'What are you drinking?'

'Vin blanc cassis.'

'I'll have the same.'

It was not yet quite the hour when most people took their midday apéritif and the Café Corneille was by no means crowded. Gautier was glad to have found Duthrey there alone because it would give him an opportunity of talking undisturbed with the journalist, whom he had not seen since the night of Sophie Monterant's death.

'I'm not asking you to give away any secrets,' Duthrey said, 'but how are you getting on with the Monterant affair?'

'I'm almost beginning to regret that I came to her apartment with you that night.'

'Because if you'd stayed away you would not have been involved in the investigation?'

'Precisely.'

'It's as bad as that?'

'You knew Monterant. Who do you think might have wished her dead?'

Duthrey thought for a few moments before replying. 'It would have to be someone in the theatre, I should think.'

'What makes you think that?'

'A few years ago a well-known actress was sent a box of marrons glacés in which fish-hooks had been implanted. I believe whoever poisoned Monterant took their idea from that incident, only they didn't merely want to wound her, they intended to finish her off.'

'Did the police ever discover who sent the fish-hooks?'

'Never. Another actress, Régine Martial, was put on trial but acquitted for lack of evidence.'

Duthrey's theory, Gautier decided, was interesting but of little practical value. The theatre was a closed and inbred society; everyone knew everyone else, had acted with them, written for them, directed them or slept with them. But it was also a very large society with many theatres, scores of actors and innumerable stagehands, dressers, programme sellers. Thousands of people must have heard about Régine Martial and the fish-hooks.

'Changing the subject completely,' he said to Duthrey, 'how much do you know about the Minister of Beaux-arts?'

'Charvet? Nothing that isn't public knowledge.'

'Is it true that he may be the next President of France?'

Duthrey took out a cigar and lit it before he replied. He was a methodical man who liked to marshal his thoughts when he was asked for his opinion on any subject of importance and would give his answer in an orderly and logical form. Gautier often thought he would have made an excellent lawyer.

Finally Duthrey said: 'We should ask ourselves what qualities the French expect in their chief of state. Look back over the last thirty years. What sort of men have occupied the Elysée Palace? A dim-witted soldier, a dishonest lawyer, a rich bourgeois, a flashy little womanizer and our current president who looks for all the world as though he had just stepped off a train from the provinces.'

Gautier laughed. Although after the fall of Napoleon III the French had been determined to create and maintain a republic, the country had shown little respect for the office of chief of state. Some presidents had been mocked, others reviled, one assassinated. Stories about each of them had been eagerly circulated with sadistic pleasure.

Maréchal MacMahon, the soldier, was not a great intellect. The story about him was that when visiting a military hospital and being shown a patient with typhoid, he remarked: 'A terrible illness, typhoid! I know because I've had it. It either kills you or it leaves you half-witted.'

Jules Grévy, the lawyer, was parsimonious, and receptions at the Elysée Palace were notoriously frugal. A young man arrested for stealing bread was supposed to have defended himself by telling the police: 'I'd just returned from dining with the president.' But Grévy had been forced to resign when it was discovered that his son-in-law had made a business out of selling honours.

Félix Faure was found dying of apoplexy, still clutching his naked mistress, Marguerite Steinheil. Casimir-Perrir was forced out of office by his unpopularity, Sadi Carnot had been stabbed to death by an anarchist, and crowds had thrown dung at Emile Loubet.

'Nevertheless, I believe that France, by trial and error, is discovering what kind of president she wants,' Duthrey continued. 'He must above all else be a good Frenchman, honest, hard-working, not too clever, good-looking without being an Adonis, liberal in his views without being a radical.'

'Does Henri Charvet fit that description?'

'Up to a point, yes.'

'But what about his wife? I get the impression that Madame Charvet has an eye for the men.'

'That does no harm. A pretty, flirtatious wife is an asset to a president,' Duthrey replied. 'Frenchmen don't expect their chief of state to set a high moral tone. Sadi Carnot tried to do so and look what happened to him. No, Charvet has only one major failing which is that he's a dull dog. If only he had run a mistress or two when he was younger or made a play for the ballerinas at the Opéra, he would be more popular.'

'Hasn't he?'

'If he has, then he's been very skilful at disguising the fact. And that would be bad. A good Frenchman should flaunt his mistresses a little, wear them like a flower in his buttonhole.'

Gautier recalled that he had heard Adèle Charvet express not dissimilar views only a short time previously. He doubted, though, whether Duthrey would share Madame Charvet's belief that women should be allowed the same sexual freedom as men. At heart the journalist was old-fashioned and the liberal beliefs which he sometimes expounded were superficial, a thin layer of icing on the good solid cake of bourgeois conservatism.

'Why this interest in the Minister of Beaux-arts?' Duthrey asked.

'I happened to meet him last night.'

'Ah, then you must have been at the Comtesse de Limousin's musical soirée.'

'How do you know?'

'It is reported in *Figaro*. As you must be aware, we carry regular news of all social events, receptions, balls, dinner-parties. We even publish a list of the days on which prominent hostesses are at home to callers.'

'You must have space to spare!'

'Not at all. That's what sells newspapers; that and the latest murder.'

Gautier sensed that Duthrey was expecting that he would explain why he had been at the home of the Limousins. Inspectors of the Sûreté were not normally received in society. Yet he was reluctant to start recounting the chain of events that had led to his taking Clémentine Lyse to the soirée. So to avoid an explanation he said: 'You know of course that the Comte de Limousin was one of Monterant's admirers?'

'Yes, that too has been reported in the gossip pages of the newspapers.'

'We had a short talk, the comte and I.'

'He is a particularly unpleasant specimen, a man too proud to mix with the bourgeoisie but not too proud to marry for money.' Duthrey paused. He had clearly realized that Gautier's talk with the comte had been linked with the death of Sophie Monterant and did not wish that his next remark should be taken as an accusation. 'The comte is a man of a most violent temper.'

'Really?'

'You may have heard that in spite of the fact that he was proposed for membership by a duke of royal blood and a former president of the Jockey Club he was refused entry to that institution. I can tell you why he was blackballed. Only a week before he came up for membership, he lost his temper with one of his grooms and whipped the man almost to the point of death. That was behaviour which the gentlemen of the equestrian world were not prepared to tolerate.'

While Duthrey was speaking a young lawyer, one of their regular companions at the Café Corneille, arrived to join them at their table. The Corneille was popular among lawyers, who liked to saunter across the river from the Palais de Justice during the mid-day adjournment of cases.

'I enjoyed your article about La Monterant,' the lawyer said to Duthrey after he had sat down with them. 'It gave a vivid, but very fair picture of the woman.'

'Thank you.'

'It was not just by coincidence, one supposes, that you described how Madame Lafitte had threatened to shoot her a year ago.'

'What do you mean?'

The lawyer nodded towards Gautier. 'I assumed it might have been a plan you two concocted to flush out the person who sent Monterant the poisoned chocolates.'

'Wait a minute!' Gautier interposed. 'Are you suggesting that it was the general's wife who sent them?'

'Didn't she?'

'We have no reason to believe so.'

'Then why did she do it?'

'Do what?'

The lawyer looked first at Gautier and then at Duthrey in surprise. 'Has neither of you heard? Madame Lafitte hanged herself at Dr Martin's place in Passy last night.'

13

'ARE YOU COMPLETELY mad, Gautier?' Courtrand demanded furiously. 'Have you abandoned reason, sense, prudence?'

'What have I done, Monsieur?'

'What have you done!' In his anger Courtrand banged on his desk and a little ink spurted out of his silver ink-well on to a sheaf of papers. 'You go to the house of one of the richest and most influential men in France to question him about the murder of some disreputable actress. If that is your notion of how an inspector of mine should act, then perhaps it's time, Gautier, that you were returned to mundane duties in a police arrondissement.'

'The Comte de Limousin was one of Madame Monterant's financial backers.'

'That does not give you the right to question him.'

'She was also his mistress.'

Courtrand looked at him sharply. 'How do you know?'

'Monterant left a diary. Besides, his wife as good as admitted it to me. And it was the comtesse who invited me to the musical evening at their home.'

The expression on Courtrand's face when he heard this was almost comical, a combination of astonishment and envy. It was as though a devout Catholic had learnt that an atheist had been granted an audience by the pope. He picked up a sheet of note-paper from his desk and waved it at Gautier.

'In that case, why has the comte written to me complaining of your high-handed behaviour?'

'I couldn't say, Monsieur le Directeur. But if you don't believe me you may ask the comtesse.'

Frustrated, Courtrand shifted his attack. 'And there's another far more serious matter. I understand you went to badger the wife of General Lafitte with questions at Dr Martin's maison de santé.'

'I spoke with her there after obtaining the permission of the doctor in charge.'

'Do you know she killed herself last night?'

'Yes, and I was very sorry to hear it. She was a very agreeable woman. But she can't possibly have killed herself on account of anything I said to her.'

'No? I wish I were as confident as you.' Courtrand's anger began to mount again. 'Holy Mother of God, Gautier! What made you decide to question her of all people?'

'She had to be one of the first suspects. You know she threatened to shoot Monterant only eighteen months ago?'

Once again Courtrand was astounded. It was clear that he had not heard this piece of Paris scandal and the incident might well have occurred when he was out of the country attending one of the international conferences of police chiefs, at which he was much in demand as a speaker. Briefly Gautier filled him in with the details.

'In spite of what you say,' Courtrand remarked when he had finished, 'it would not surprise me at all if General Lafitte made a formal complaint to the Prefect of Police.'

'On what grounds?'

'You should have sought his authority before questioning Madame Lafitte, surely you can see that? In fact, Gautier, I have decided that as a matter of courtesy the general must receive an apology from the Sûreté.'

Gautier was not surprised at Courtrand's decision. The director's appointment had been one of political patronage and he repaid it with an obsequious regard for everyone who had the slightest political importance.

'And it is you who will make the apology, as I'm sure you will agree is only proper,' Courtrand continued. 'I have already made an appointment for you to go and see General Lafitte.'

'When?'

'He has said he will see you this afternoon at four o'clock at the Cercle Militaire in Rue de Rivoli.'

The instructions and the tone in which they were given were clearly meant as a reprimand but Gautier was in no way upset. General Lafitte was one of the people whom he had planned to interview and Courtrand had made an opportunity for him to do just that. He had a feeling that if any of Sophie Monterant's admirers were implicated in her death it would be the general. Army officers, he had found, did not have a very high regard for human life and were trained to be accustomed to violence. He turned to leave the room.

'Before you go, Inspector,' Courtrand said, 'I have to tell you that I am far from satisfied with the way in which you are handling the investigation into the death of this woman, Monterant. As far as I can see, you have been concentrating your enquiries entirely among people of wealth and importance who happened to know the dead woman.'

'Yes, Sir. Because I believe they must be involved.'

The director-general rose from his desk and began to pace up and down the room, plainly irritated. 'What in heaven is wrong with you, man?' he grumbled. 'Do you really imagine that people of good social position and influence would send poisoned chocolates to some actress?'

'I don't rule out the possibility.'

'Then you should. My dear Gautier, Monterant was a woman of doubtful morals. She belonged to the demi-monde and that's where you'll find the person who killed her; someone in the theatre whom she had wronged or a woman whose lover she stole or even a servant who bore her a grudge.'

'I don't believe so,' Gautier said stubbornly.

'And what of the woman whom the newspapers are hinting was the one who sent the poisoned chocolates? Have you questioned her yet?'

'Yes,' Gautier replied and he could not resist adding: 'She's the singer, Clémentine Lyse, and you may as well know that it was she who accompanied me as my partner to the Comtesse de Limousin's soireé last night.'

This time Courtrand kept his surprise and his anger under control. Without speaking he went to the window and flung it open. For a Frenchman, even in the month of May, to admit fresh air voluntarily into his office, was a sign of desperation. Gautier wondered whether perhaps some primitive instinct was warning Courtrand that his body needed oxygen to combat the danger of asphyxiation through rage.

Finally Courtrand said quietly: 'I have allowed you latitude in the past, Gautier, and because you have used it wisely and to advantage, I shall allow you latitude on this occasion; but not unlimited latitude. If you have no results to report to me within twenty-four hours, this woman Lyse will be brought in for questioning. If necessary a juge d'instruction will be appointed to interrogate her and such other people as he thinks fit.'

'I understand.'

'Twenty-four hours, no more. In the meantime kindly remember that General Lafitte is expecting you at four o'clock this afternoon.'

The Cercle Militaire was a club for past and present army officers, modelled on the clubs in London which afforded English gentlemen an escape from the company of vulgar persons in trade and from their ladies. Although the ordinary people of France still nursed an almost paranoiac hatred of the British, the upper classes could not stop imitating English manners, dress and institutions, foxhunting, smoking jackets and tyrannical children's governesses.

The club's premises were on the first and upper floors of a building in Rue de Rivoli, overlooking the Tuileries gardens. Gautier was told by a club servant that General Lafitte was waiting for him in the library which, presumably to remind members that soldiers were men of deeds and not words, was a very small room with very few books: dictionaries to help members with their spelling, an atlas or two with which to plan future campaigns, and half-a-dozen volumes on military strategy to recapture the glories of the past. The club committee, thoughtfully, had also provided deep leather armchairs in which a warrior could doze for a while to recover from the exertions of reading.

General Lafitte was a short, broad man with gentle eyes, thinning hair and a beautifully cultivated moustache. He was seated in one of the leather armchairs, cradling a large glass of cognac in his hands.

After he had introduced himself, Gautier said: 'I was desolate to hear of the death of Madame Lafitte.'

'Please sit down, Inspector,' the general replied. 'Yes, it was a great shock, even though not altogether unexpected.'

'Did you know that I went to see her in Passy two days ago?'

'Yes, to talk to her about the death of Sophie Monterant.'

'Perhaps I should not have gone.'

'Don't reproach yourself, Inspector. My wife's suicide was not occasioned by your visit. She didn't kill Sophie.'

'I realized that after I had spoken with her.'

The general shrugged his shoulders. 'Still, it was understandable that you should have suspected her after that farcical business with the shotgun.'

'As a matter of fact, General, I never really supposed that your wife had sent Madame Monterant the poisoned chocolates.'

'No? Then whom did you suspect.'

'You.'

The statement did not disconcert the general as much as Gautier had expected. All he said was: 'What reason would I have for killing Sophie? You must know, of course, that she and I were lovers.'

'Wouldn't it be more correct to say "had been" lovers? I understand she transferred her affections to the Comte de Limousin some weeks ago.'

The general sipped his cognac reflectively and looked out of the windows across the Tuileries gardens. A class of schoolchildren escorted by a teacher had just crossed Rue de Rivoli in a double file and was going down the steps into the gardens in search of open air. Since their defeat by Germany thirty-odd years previously, the French had been obsessed with the need to improve the nation's physique, and exercise had become part of the curriculum in many schools.

'It's strange,' General Lafitte was thinking aloud, 'I feel no grief for Sophie now. When she began her affair with the comte, I was mad with jealousy. I could not conceive that I would be able to live without her. But now that she is dead, I feel nothing except a calm and tranquillity that I have not known for two years or more. It is as though a malignant growth has been cut out of my life.

Now I reproach myself part of the time for my callous indifference and part of the time for not having realized months ago what I should have done.'

'Left her, you mean?'

'That would have solved nothing. No, Inspector, I should have done what my wife was ready to do for my sake and what I would never have had the courage to do. I should have killed Sophie.' He looked at Gautier and smiled sadly. 'Does that answer the question you wished to ask me?'

'Yes, I believe it does.'

It was not in the words of the general that Gautier had found his answer, but in his eyes and in his manner. They were the eyes and manner of an indecisive and gentle man; a man too gentle for military greatness, too gentle for a love affair with a hard, demanding woman, too gentle to have killed her.

He left the general in the club, with a glass of cognac to colour his dreams of campaigns he had never waged, of women he had never dominated, of decisions he had never made. As he went, frustrated, down the stairs and into the sunlit Rue de Rivoli, Gautier said aloud, more in anger than in pity: 'Another wasted life!'

14

WHEN GAUTIER ARRIVED at the house where Sophie Monterant had lived he found the concierge with not one but two crawling children in her charge. Her ill temper had not, as one might have expected, increased in proportion to this additional responsibility. Instead she was at ease, almost benign as she allowed the two grandchildren to attack each other and the furniture with abandon, while she continued with her knitting.

In answer to Gautier's enquiry she told him that the maid, Françoise, was not at home but out looking for another place. The relatives of Madame Monterant, according to the concierge, had told Françoise that they would not be employing her, nor had any provision been made for her in the will of the actress. It was scandalous that an old servant, who had served her mistress so faithfully, should be abandoned in this callous way, but that was the only treatment working folk could expect.

'When do you expect her to return?' Gautier asked.

'It is surprising that she's not back already. She only went to Rue de Courcelles.'

'Rue de Courcelles!' Gautier exclaimed. 'Do you by any chance know whom she went to see?'

'A lady who said she might be able to help her find a place. She's a singer. I don't know her name, but she's well known in the neighbourhood as a kind person who is always ready to help anyone in need. Why, she has kept some poor families from starving with her charity these past three years! When she heard Françoise was out of work she even sent her carriage round here to fetch her this afternoon.'

One of the two infants screamed. Although neither of them

could have been more than a few months old, the larger, a girl, had managed to drag herself upright and was standing precariously but triumphantly, with most of her weight on the boy's hand. She's started, Gautier thought cynically, as no doubt she'll go through life, treading some male into the dust.

'I know the lady you mean,' Gautier told the concierge as she went to rescue the small boy. 'And I think I'll go and see what has become of Françoise.' The knowledge that Clémentine was interesting herself in the future of Françoise made him uneasy.

'There's no need,' replied the concierge, looking out of the window. 'Unless I'm mistaken, this is her returning and the lady's with her.'

A carriage, which Gautier recognized as one of those owned by Clémentine, had stopped outside the house. Françoise and Clémentine got down from it and stood talking outside. Gautier left the conciergerie, and the two women looked round as he approached them.

'Are you looking for me, Inspector?' Clémentine asked.

'I came to see Françoise, Madame, but I also have a message for you.'

'I'll go and wait upstairs in the apartment, Monsieur,' Françoise said and then turning towards Clémentine she added: 'I must thank you again, Madame, for finding a place for me. It was very good of you.'

When she had gone, Clémentine faced Gautier. There was nothing in her manner to suggest that she even remembered the suggestion he made to her the previous night when his desire had been aroused, or the anger it had provoked in her.

'And what is this message which you have for me?' she asked.

'I simply wished to warn you that either tomorrow or the following day, I may be compelled to ask you to come to Sûreté headquarters.'

'I see. Is this your way of revenging yourself?'

'If I had wanted revenge, I could have taken you there for questioning this morning, even last night.'

'Then why have you decided to do so now?'

Gautier explained to her that it was not his decision, that the

Director of the Sûreté was dissatisfied with the progress that was being made in the enquiries and that Gautier had been given twenty-four hours to pursue his own ideas. At the end of that time, everyone who might be connected with the death of Sophie Monterant would be questioned at headquarters, in all probability by a juge d'instruction. After he had finished speaking, Clémentine was silent for several seconds. Then she said quietly: 'If that happens it will be the end of my career, you know that?'

'Aren't you exaggerating?'

'Have you not heard of what happened to Régine Martial?'

'Yes, but she was a little-known actress. You have a following of thousands.'

'But for how long? Already they are beginning to turn against me. Last night there were even some who booed me at the Eldorado.'

'You forget that nobody ever did find out who sent the marrons glacés to Régine Martial's rival. Once we establish who poisoned Monterant all this hysteria will soon be forgotten.'

'Ah, but will you find out who killed her?'

'Of course we will.' Gautier was surprised at the confidence in his tone and even more surprised to realize that he was not dissembling. He really did believe that the Monterant affair would be solved.

She touched his arm, as though she were apprehensive and hoped to find reassurance in physical contact, however slight. 'Will you tell me as soon as you have any news? To be kept waiting in suspense, not knowing what is happening, is more than I can endure.'

'Certainly I will.'

'You know where I live.' Her lips twitched in what may have been meant to be a smile. 'You'll be welcome at any time—day or night.'

Turning away abruptly, she climbed back into her carriage. Gautier watched as the coachman drove it away. Was what she had just said another invitation, he wondered, or an expression of regret for her outburst the previous night, or even both. He went upstairs to Sophie Monterant's apartment, glad that now he was going to be dealing with an uncomplicated countrywoman who would not confuse their discussion with ambiguities and half-truths. Françoise was waiting for him.

'When I saw you after your mistress's death,' he said to her, 'I told you that on no account were you to tell anyone of your suspicion that Mademoiselle Lyse might have sent the poisoned chocolates, but you disregarded my instructions and told newspaper reporters.' Françoise stared at him sullenly but said nothing. He continued: 'That's true, isn't it?'

'Yes, Monsieur.'

'Well, your stupidity has got you into trouble, as I warned you it might. Before long one of my assistants will be coming here to take you to appear before a juge d'instruction to repeat those accusations.'

'But Monsieur, I know now that Mademoiselle Clémentine did not kill the mistress!'

'How do you know?'

'I've met her. And everyone, the concierge in her house and all the servants, say she's a saint. Look what she has done for me.'

Gautier realized that it had clearly never occurred to Françoise that Clémentine Lyse might have heard that it was Monterant's maid who had been accusing her and found her a position simply in order that she would withdraw the accusations.

'Anyway, it was a man who brought the chocolates to the house,' Françoise added, 'not a woman.'

'How do you know that?'

'The concierge told me.'

'When I asked her she told me it was a boy.'

'Well, that isn't what she is saying now.'

As he went down the stairs, Gautier felt a quickening excitement. What Françoise had told him was trivial enough but it offered the first link, however tenuous, with the unknown sender of the poisoned chocolates. Concierges were as a breed inquisitive and observant; it was their business to know other people's business. The one in this house, he was certain, knew more than she had been prepared to tell him when he had first questioned her. When he reached the conciergerie he found her still there with the two children, who were growing progressively grubbier.

'Some days ago, Madame, I asked you about a parcel which had been delivered here on the day Madame Monterant died.'

'Yes, the poisoned chocolates.'

'You told me then that the parcel had been delivered to you in the evening. Is that true?'

His question did not please the concierge. She replied sullenly: 'No. I remembered later that it was given to me quite early in the afternoon.'

'But you didn't give it to Madame Monterant immediately?'

'If I rushed upstairs every time she got a parcel or a love letter, it would be the death of me. Anyway, I knew that she was at the theatre that afternoon rehearsing. So I put the parcel on one side and forgot it till I gave it to her maid later.'

'I see. And who brought the parcel here?'

'A man.'

'Are you sure of that?'

'Yes, quite certain.'

'Can you describe him?'

'Oh, he was a gentleman. I remember noticing that. Very smartly dressed and handsome too, in a foreign sort of way.'

Gautier remembered that he was still carrying the photograph of Marcel Pelotti in his pocket. He showed it to the concierge.

'Would that be the man by any chance?'

'Why, yes, Monsieur! That's him without any doubt.'

Shortly after mid-day next day, Inspector Lemaire came into Gautier's office and handed him a document. It was a copy of a report, now in the official dossier of the murder of Lucie Bertron, and Courtrand had decided that Gautier should receive one. He read it through.

MINISTRY OF JUSTICE

Death by violence of Mlle L. Bertron   Dossier No. 0139

This day, 28 May, we Rolland had brought before us the prisoner Marcel Pelotti. Our examination of him was as follows:

Question: Pelotti, you have already admitted being responsible for the illegal killing of the woman, Lucie Bertron. Today I propose to question you about another affair. What do you know about the death of the actress, Sophie Monterant?

Pelotti: Absolutely nothing, Sir.

Question: Are you saying that you have never heard of her?

Pelotti: Oh, I've heard of her. What educated person in Paris hasn't?

Question: Do you know where she lived?

Pelotti: No, Sir. I do not.

Question: Then how is it that you delivered a parcel addressed to Madame Monterant at her house.

Pelotti: You must be mistaken. It was not me.

Question: Come, Pelotti, don't waste any more of my time with your useless denials. The concierge at the building has identified you as the man who delivered the parcel. In that parcel, it has been established, was a box containing poisoned chocolates and later the same evening Madame Monterant ate one of them and died. Do you deny that you were responsible for her death?

Pelotti: I do, most emphatically.

Question: Let us start again. Did you deliver a parcel to the house?

Pelotti: I do not remember doing so.

Question: But the concierge has identified you as the man who did. (No reply from the prisoner) Let me ask you once more. Were you the person who delivered the parcel?

Pelotti: If the concierge says so, I suppose I must have been.

Question: And you knew the parcel contained a box of chocolates?

Pelotti: Yes. All right, I did know.

Question: Then how can you say you did not cause Madame Monterant's death? (No reply) I shall put the questions to you once more. Did you take the parcel of chocolates to the house?

Pelotti: Yes.

Question: Did you know the parcel was intended for Madame Monterant?

Pelotti: Yes.

Question: And you knew the chocolates had been poisoned? (No reply) I put it to you that it is inconceivable you did not know. (No reply) Why do you persist in this stubbornness? By your own admission you killed the woman Bertron. You will be adjudged guilty of her murder and punished accordingly. What do you hope to gain by denying that you did not also kill Madame Monterant?

Pelotti: What you are saying is that I can only be taken to the guillotine once.

Question: They are your words, not mine.

Pelotti: All right, let's put an end to this farce. I admit I took the chocolates to the house.

Question: Knowing full well that they were poisoned?

Pelotti: Yes.

Question: Ah, so you confess! And did you also put the poison in the chocolates?

Pelotti: Me? What do I know of poisoning? I'm not a common assassin. No, I paid someone else to do it.

Question: Who?

Pelotti: That I shall never tell you. Do you imagine that I am completely without honour? As you know there are plenty of people in Paris who will perform a little task like that if the price is right. But I warn you, I will never reveal the name of the person who aided me, whatever you may do. I have my reputation to consider.

Question: Are you asking us to believe that there is honour among scoundrels and criminals like you?

Pelotti: I can tell you, Monsieur le Juge, one will find more honour and honesty among what you describe as the scoundrels of Paris than in the corridors of the Ministry of Justice.

Question: All right, we will leave that matter aside for the present. Now I would like to know why you wished to kill Madame Monterant.

Pelotti: Are my reasons important?

Question: They may provide extenuating circumstances which will be taken into account when judgment is passed on you.

Pelotti: I see. You mean I may be guillotined only once and not twice.

Question: This impertinence will not help your cause. I ask you again. Why did you kill Madame Monterant?

Pelotti: I notice that you always refer to her, disreputable actress though she was, as 'Madame', but poor Lucie is only 'the woman Bertron'. Why does Monterant deserve this honour? They were both whores, in your eyes at least.

Question: Just answer my questions and remember it is I who am conducting this examination.

Pelotti: Shall we say I killed her for revenge?

Question: Revenge? For what?

Pelotti: I forget.

Question: It is ridiculous to suggest that anyone could fail to remember why they killed a woman.

Pelotti: Well, it was months ago, but I do remember now. She persuaded me to spend a night with her, even though I didn't wish to. Then in the morning she threw me out, without even giving me a present, saying that what I had given her was not worth any reward. I have never been so insulted in my life.

Question: Are you saying that you slept with women for money?

Pelotti: Certainly not! But if they insisted on showing their gratitude with a present, who am I to deprive them of that pleasure. It was not them whom I made pay, but their husbands. And why not? I was giving their wives something they could not give.

Question: Are you saying that you were prepared to blackmail the husbands of these women?

Pelotti: Call it what you like, Monsieur le Juge. I think of it as a just reward for services rendered.

Question: And when did this business take place? When do you claim to have spent a night with Madame Monterant?

Pelotti: It must have been a month ago. Yes, almost exactly a month.

Question: A short while back you said it had happened months ago. Are you now changing your story?

Pelotti: One month, two months, several. What does it matter?

Question: We will question you further on that subject. For the present will you admit again that you took the chocolates to

Madame Monterant's apartment, knowing that they were poisoned and intending to do her harm?
Pelotti: Yes, I meant to kill her.

Signed:

Rolland
Courtrand
Lemaire

As he read the account of Pelotti's examination, Gautier felt somehow disappointed. He had expected that the Italian would have made, if not an outright denial of the concierge's accusation, then at least a more ingenious explanation for what he had done, a more spirited defence. Pelotti had given the impression of being a man with a certain style, even dignity, who would not have lowered himself to revenge a slight by one woman when there were apparently so many others ready to appreciate his sexual talents.

'How did Pelotti behave during the examination?' he asked Lemaire. 'Obviously he was not over-awed by Judge Rolland and the director.'

'Exactly the opposite! I couldn't help admiring his cheek. And as for the answers he gave to Rolland's questions, he seemed ready to admit to almost anything, just to get the whole business over. Oh, he's a cool one, all right.'

'It is almost as though he were in a hurry to get to the guillotine.'

'Anyway, now that he's confessed that's an end to it.'

'Apparently so.'

'Courtrand asked me to remind you that he said the person who killed Monterant would be found among the riff-raff of Paris.'

'And he's been proved right.' Gautier smiled. 'That should put him in a good temper.'

'He strutted up and down the room, puffed up with pride. But that didn't stop him asking me to give you an instruction you won't like.'

'What's that?'

Lemaire told him that an exhibition of paintings was to be officially opened that afternoon at the Salle Delacroix by the

122

Minister of Beaux-arts. An anonymous letter had been received by the ministry, warning them that there would be a political disturbance at the ceremony. The Prefect of Police had given instructions that the Sûreté should take the necessary precautions.

'And Courtrand is taking the opportunity to put me in my place. He knows it will all come to nothing.'

'Oh, it wasn't Courtrand who chose you,' Lemaire said. 'It seems that the Minister of Beaux-arts asked specially that you should be put in charge.'

15

THE SALLE DELACROIX was a newly-constructed and lavish art gallery just off the Champs Elysées in Avenue de Marigny. Gautier could remember it being officially opened by the then President of France, Félix Faure, not many years previously.

The exhibition at which he was on duty that afternoon was a collection of paintings organized by the Ministry of Beaux-arts under the title 'Masters of French Art'. The pictures had been assembled from museums, public buildings and galleries all over France, as well as from private collections, and they represented the work of the great established artists of the last twenty years: Meissonier and Détaille, the masters of military subjects and famous battles; Cormon who specialized in pre-historic scenes; Jean-Paul Laurens who won a reputation for painting executions; Bourguereau the painter of voluptuous nudes; Béraud whose scenes of contemporary life in Paris had won a large following; and the fashionable portrait painters, Bonnat and Duran.

The newspapers had announced that the exhibition was meant to be a reaffirmation of the superiority of the 'chers maîtres' who had reigned supreme in France for the last thirty years over the vulgar and sensational aspirations of the so-called new art movements.

Gautier had arrived at the gallery early and posted half-a-dozen policemen at strategic points inside the building. Then he had confirmed with the organizing officials that all invitations would be carefully checked and no one admitted to the exhibition who was not in possession of one. The main gallery in the building was a long, rectangular room which opened into smaller rooms at each side in which more pictures were on display. At the far end of the main gallery were offices and a kitchen in which the food and drink to be served at the 'vernissage' or opening reception would be prepared and brought to guests by waiters. A platform from which the minister would speak had been erected next to the door leading to the offices. As a precaution Gautier had made a tour of the entire premises to make certain that no intruders could have entered the gallery earlier that day and found themselves a hiding place.

By the time he had finished his inspection, the guests who had been invited to the vernissage were beginning to arrive. They included foreign diplomats, senior government officials, patrons of art, a sprinkling from the aristocracy and art critics from the leading newspapers and magazines, just over 300 people in all. Among the arrivals Gautier recognized the Comte and Comtesse de Limousin, accompanied by the comtesse's beautiful secretary. Few of the guests appeared to take more than a casual interest in the paintings hanging from the walls of the gallery. Instead most of them stood gossiping and drinking the champagne which the waiters were carrying round, while they waited for the official opening ceremony.

At four o'clock the Minister of Beaux-arts and Madame Charvet arrived in an open landau. They were met at the entrance to the gallery by the owner of the Salle Delacroix, the President of the Académie des Beaux-arts, who had assisted in the selection of the paintings on display, and a senior civil servant from the ministry.

Once inside the main gallery, the official party began a tour of the exhibition. As unobtrusively as he could Gautier slipped in between them and the small crowd which was following them round. From time to time the minister would stop to study a painting and make some observation about it. Elsewhere he would recognize someone in the crowd of guests and would pause to exchange a few words. At one point he stopped to admire a canvas by Bourguereau. Entitled 'La Bacchante', it depicted a rather fleshy naked girl lying on the ground and smilingly fondling a goat, which appeared to be about to leap over her. Like all Bourguereau's work it was a laborious composition, vulgar in its colouring, sentimental but at the same time suggestive. Although the critics had never loved the artist, the public did and he had become one of the wealthiest of the 'chers maîtres' of the Belle Epoque, producing at least twenty major compositions each year and calculating that he was earning a hundred francs for every minute which he spent at his easel.

'What superb composition!' the minister exclaimed. His remarks were neither original nor perceptive. 'And look at the detail! What delicate brushwork!'

Madame Charvet, who had been following one pace behind her husband on his tour, quietly stepped back a further pace, so that she was standing right in front of Gautier. He could feel her skirt brushing against his legs and was aware once again of her perfume.

Without turning her head, she said: 'And what do you think of the painting, Inspector?'

It took Gautier a few seconds to realize that the remark was addressed to him. 'It's a little too large for my drawing-room, Madame.'

'Really? And what about the lady? Isn't she a little too large for your taste?'

'Possibly. But not for my drawing-room.'

She laughed and said: 'I wondered if perhaps you were envying the goat.'

As the official party moved on, the smile she gave him was both suggestive and conspiratorial. Anyone seeing it might have supposed they were already lovers and Gautier hoped it had passed unnoticed.

At the end of his tour, the minister mounted the platform at the end of the main gallery. It was from there that he was to make the speech formally opening the exhibition, after which he and the more important guests would retire into one of the offices to drink their champagne away from the crowds.

First the President of the Académie des Beaux-arts, himself an artist of the traditional school, famous for his paintings of scenes taken from classical mythology, introduced the minister. Then Charvet spoke. Listening to him, Gautier noticed a remarkable similarity between the speech the minister was making today and what he had said to Gautier at the soirée of the Comtesse de Limousin. On that occasion he had been talking about the theatre, this time it was art, but many of the phrases he used and the sentiments he expressed about the work of his ministry and the cultural leadership of France were identical.

'We live in a restless world,' Charvet declared, 'and there are people who, through restlessness and an awareness of their own mediocrity, would force change on us. Art, we are told, must no longer depict the beautiful nor seek to imitate the incomparable art of nature. Instead, these philistines say, artists must express what they are thinking and what they feel, no matter how squalid or purposeless. Nor need they learn the skills of drawing or composition or colour. All they need to do is to pick up a paintbrush and daub the canvas in a manner that defies comprehension. If that is modern art, my friends, if that is its philosophy, then let us be glad that France still has her traditional painters, the men who have painted and are still painting the great homeric canvases, the wonderful landscapes, the unforgettable moments of history, the splendid, life-like portraits that we are privileged to enjoy in this fine exhibition.'

Gautier wondered how the art critics in the audience must be reacting to Charvet's words. Over the last few years the popularity of the 'chers maîtres' had been rapidly waning in the world of art. Critics wrote disparagingly of their works, calling them by the derisive name of 'pompiers', and praising instead the new schools of impressionism, post-impressionism and symbolism. But whatever the critics might think, the guests at the vernissage appeared to enjoy Charvet's speech and when he finished they applauded him handsomely. He bowed and began to leave the platform.

Two steps led down from the platform to the floor and as Charvet walked down them a man stepped forward from the crowd. He was a small man, bald but with neatly waxed moustaches and beard, impeccably dressed and carrying a straw hat, as were many of the other guests that day. When he held out his free hand towards the minister, Gautier thought at first that he was offering Charvet his congratulations on the speech.

Then the man called out in a high-pitched voice: 'I come to revenge our gallant soldiers who have perished in North Africa. You, Monsieur, are the government and therefore you too must die.'

Only then did Gautier realize that the man was holding a revolver in his outstretched hand. Charvet had stopped, one foot on the floor, one still on a step, his features fixed in a grimace of disbelief at the sight of the gun. Swiftly, in what was almost a reflex action, Gautier stepped forward, placing himself protectively in front of the minister, facing the would-be assassin.

'Get out of the way!' the man screamed. 'You and I have no quarrel. It is the government I have to destroy.'

'You will destroy no one, Monsieur,' Gautier said firmly. 'Give me that pistol.'

'Get out of the way!'

The man straightened his arm until the muzzle of the revolver was no more than half a metre away from Gautier. His hand was steady, his eyes defiant. This, Gautier knew, was a sign of danger, an indication that the man was capable of killing. He realized that if he grabbed for the revolver there was a good chance that he could knock the muzzle away, but even so, if the trigger was squeezed there would still be a bullet, flying off wildly to kill or maim some innocent person in the crowd.

'Give me that pistol, Monsieur,' he repeated.

For what seemed like minutes the two of them stared at each other. The whole gallery was frozen in silence. Then a muscle at one corner of the man's left eye began to twitch, his hand shook almost imperceptibly and Gautier knew that the danger had passed.

He reached out slowly and the man allowed him to take the revolver from his grasp. Immediately two uniformed policemen who had been moving silently into position behind him, rushed forward, seized the man and twisted his arms behind his back.

'Take him outside to the wagon,' Gautier told them.

The silence in the gallery was suddenly shattered, like a sheet of glass, into a thousand fragments of excited noise. Charvet was still standing, motionless, paralysed it seemed, on the steps half-way down from the platform. At a sign from Gautier two of his aides from the ministry hurried forward, helped him down and led him out of the gallery into one of the offices at the back. After a moment of indecision, the President of the Académie led the principal guests in after them and Gautier followed.

Inside the office Charvet found words to express his feelings. Turning on Gautier he shouted hysterically: 'You were supposed to prevent that outrage. Incompetent imbecile! How dare you put my life in danger?' Then he looked at his wife, his lips still

128

trembling with a compound of rage and fear. 'Your whims are becoming too costly, Adèle. Your insatiable lust is getting past endurance. This was your fault.'

Madame Charvet looked at him with indifference and said calmly: 'When you've recovered from your pitiful cowardice, Henri, you'll be sorry that you didn't keep silent.'

Charvet was not ready to listen to reason or prudence. Again he stormed at Gautier: 'The Prefect of Police will hear of this. This is the last time you'll be allowed to mix with your betters, you can count on that.'

'Don't you think you're being unfair, Minister?' The Comtesse de Limousin was standing not far from Gautier and it was she who, unexpectedly, had intervened. 'After all, Inspector Gautier, by his gallantry, saved your life.'

'Thank you, Madame,' Gautier said. 'But there was no real danger. The revolver was not loaded.' The pistol was still in his possession and he held it out for everyone to see.

'But you could not possibly have known that!' the comtesse protested.

Learning that his life had not after all been in any real danger seemed only to increase Charvet's fury. He shouted at Gautier: 'What has been done with that villain? I wish to know exactly how he came to be allowed into the building in spite of the precautions which you were supposed to have arranged.'

'He has been taken outside to the police wagon.'

'Then go and make sure he is still being held. I wouldn't put it past your stupidity to allow him to escape.'

Gautier left the office and went into the main gallery. The injustice of the minister's remarks did not upset him unduly, for he was confident that neither he nor the Sûreté would be held responsible for the nasty fright which Charvet had been given that afternoon. The Prefect of Police was a fair man and well capable of dealing with temperamental politicians.

One of his uniformed policemen was standing outside the door to the office and he told Gautier that they were holding the man who had pointed the revolver at the minister in the police wagon outside.

'Do you know who he is and how he got here?' Gautier asked.

'Yes, Inspector. He's a former art teacher who was once head of the academy of art in Lyon but is now retired and living in Paris. He was sent an invitation to the vernissage by the Ministry of Beaux-arts.'

'Well, take him down to headquarters and keep him locked up. If the minister has his way there may well be an official enquiry into the incident.'

'All right, Inspector, but if you want my opinion the poor chap is harmless.'

A number of journalists who had been at the opening ceremony had gathered round the door to the office in which the minister had taken refuge. Although they had come to report on the exhibition, they now knew they had a better and more sensational story to take back to their papers. One of them, Charlus, the art editor of *Figaro* and a colleague of Duthrey, had met Gautier from time to time at the Café Corneille.

'What's happening in there, Inspector?' he asked Gautier. 'Are we going to be allowed to question the minister?'

'Perhaps when he has recovered. He's badly shaken.'

'He need not make too much of that little farce. It has happened before.'

'What do you mean?'

'That art teacher Marquet has pointed his empty pistol before at three government ministers, to my knowledge. There may have been others.'

'What's wrong with the man?'

'He's mad, of course. It seems he goes round telling people that his son was an officer in the Foreign Legion, who was wounded by Arabs and left to die in the desert. But it's all a delusion. He has never had a son.'

'Why hasn't he been locked up?'

Charlus shrugged his shoulders. 'When he retired he was given the Légion d'Honneur, so the authorities don't wish to be too hard on him. Besides he is really harmless.'

Gautier went back into the office and saw that the atmosphere was still tense and uncomfortable. Charvet had recovered his composure but not his temper and was now complaining angrily to the President of the Académie, while the senior ministry official listened nervously. Madame Charvet stood staring moodily out of a window and one sensed that she would not easily forgive her husband for his outburst. Of the guests in the room, only the Comte de Limousin appeared entirely at ease. He was with his wife, drinking champagne with his customary air of listless boredom, which on this occasion might have been edged with sardonic amusement.

'Well, Inspector,' the minister demanded, 'what has been done with that wretch?'

'He is being escorted to Sûreté headquarters and will in due course be put under lock and key.'

'I am glad to hear it. And what have you found out about him? He's an anarchist, I suppose?'

'I wouldn't think so, Monsieur le Ministre. He is a Chevalier of the Légion d'Honneur.'

'Are you being impertinent?'

Gautier explained, though not as tactfully as he might have done, that Marquet had been in effect a former employee of the Ministry of Beaux-arts and recommended for his decoration by a former minister. He could see no reason for sparing Charvet embarrassment, so he also told him that Marquet had played the same melodrama with three different ministers before, always with an unloaded pistol.

'Of course the poor fellow is suffering from delusions,' he concluded. 'He's a harmless lunatic.'

Someone in the room laughed; a laugh not of amusement, but of relief at the anti-climax. Charvet's expression of cold but controlled anger disintegrated into pure fury. Seeing that Gautier was for the moment out of his reach, he switched his assault to his subordinates, rounding on the senior official from the ministry.

'So, we have ourselves to thank for this débâcle! You permitted a man who has already attacked ministers of the state on no less than three occasions to be invited here today. Was it your deliberate intent to make a spectacle of the ministry or to make a jackass of me?'

'I'm sorry, Minister,' the wretched official began.

'You may be regretting your bungling stupidity now, but I can assure you it is nothing to the regret you'll feel when I've finished with you. How long did you have to serve before you could have claimed your pension?'

Madame Charvet turned away from her husband as though she were now amused by his behaviour. She said to Gautier lightly: 'You see what it's like to live with a politician? Poor Henri is terrified in case this might mar his chances of becoming president. But he will have forgotten the whole business by tomorrow.'

Among the ministry officials who had been in attendance on Charvet was the minister's private secretary, a man named Preule. Although he could not have been far short of forty, Preule had the face of a studious schoolboy and fat hands which he used too freely to help him express himself. He had been listening to Charvet castigate his colleague and now he stepped forward.

'Might I have a word with you, Minister?'

'What is it, Preule?'

It seemed to Gautier that Charvet's manner softened when his secretary approached him, although he was still very angry. Preule took him on one side and they spoke earnestly together out of earshot of the other officials and guests. Whatever he was being told must have pleased the minister because presently he clasped Preule's shoulder with something like affection. Then he turned to the other guests and officials.

'This young man,' he said, 'has quite rightly pointed out to me that the guests outside and the press will be expecting an explanation of that drama which they witnessed. I shall return to the gallery and make an announcement.'

He left the office followed by his entourage, his wife and the guests. As she passed where Gautier was standing Madame Charvet smiled at him. Her smile, with its promise of intimacy, made him think of one of those tropical flowers whose gaudy colours were a trap for unsuspecting insects.

Back in the main gallery, Charvet mounted the platform. Preule, who appeared to have assumed the rôle previously played by his senior colleague from the ministry, called for silence and then told the assembly that the minister had a further announcement to make. Gautier was astonished to see how quickly Charvet's manner changed now that he had rid himself of physical fear and now that he had an audience. Instinctively, easily, like a skilled actor

132

playing a familiar part, he slipped into the rôle of politician.

'My friends,' he began, 'a short time ago you all witnessed in this gallery an incident which must have alarmed and shocked you, when a man threatened my life with a pistol. Many of you will be wondering who that man was, why he should have wished to harm me and what has happened to him. Before telling you about him, I must first of all pay tribute to the unselfish courage of Inspector Gautier of the Sûreté who, as you all saw, thrust himself between the assailant and me regardless of his personal safety. We in France are indeed fortunate that we have in our police force men like Inspector Gautier, loyal, brave and determined to defend our freedom.'

Charvet paused long enough to point towards Gautier and to give his audience time to absorb and understand what he was saying. Then he continued: 'As to the man who pointed the firearm at me, he is not, as one might have reasonably supposed, an anarchist or a political malcontent. No, it will surprise you to know that this poor fellow is himself an artist, formerly professor at one of our national art academies, but now, sad to say, mentally deranged. He attacked me not through personal malice, nor for any grudge against the government, but because he is suffering from delusions. Since he is not a criminal, you will I am sure agree that it would be unthinkable that he should be sent to prison or punished in any other way, and I have given instructions that no legal process should be begun against him. Instead, I believe that he should be given the medical care that he needs. I am therefore proposing to start a subscription list to raise funds for this purpose. My own name will head the list with a donation of 1,000 francs. Would those of you who would wish to join me in this act of mercy be good enough to give your names—or better still your contributions—to officials of my ministry who will circulate amongst you for this purpose. In this way, my friends, we can ensure that this poor man, a lover of art who has served art and his country well, may be sent to a sanatorium where perhaps he can be cured of the sickness that ails his mind or, if that is not possible, where at least he can spend his remaining days in peace and dignity.'

The effect of his words on the people in the room must have

been very satisfying for the minister. When he stopped speaking, there was emotional applause and almost immediately men in the audience began reaching for their pocket-books.

Not everyone, however, had been affected by the minister's oratory. The Comte de Limousin, who had been at the back of the group of important personages with his wife, sauntered forward, beckoned to Gautier and took him on one side.

'Tell me, Inspector,' he said, 'I understand from your director that Pelotti has confessed to murdering Madame Monterant.'

'That is correct.'

'Then what, may I ask, are you proposing to do with that diary of hers?'

'It will be returned with her other possessions to the nearest relatives.'

'Madame Monterant had no close relatives. Her parents are both dead. It would be better if you handed the diary over to me.'

Immediately Gautier began to wonder whether he had missed some reference in the diary which the comte did not wish to be made public. He replied: 'I'm sorry, Monsieur, I do not have the authority to do as you ask.'

'No? From your behaviour one had formed the impression that you were the Minister of Justice himself. I can see, then, that I shall have to speak to my friend the Prefect of Police.'

16

THE CAFÉ SOLEIL D'OR, in spite of its name, was in a dark, unprepossessing street that led off Place Pigalle. It was a bistro frequented mainly by working men, unwelcoming and cheerless, although an attempt had been made to brighten it up with fresh paint and new oil-cloth on the tables.

Gautier had made his way there reluctantly in the evening after he had eaten at a restaurant near the Sûreté; reluctantly because he had no wish to meet the man with whom Suzanne was living. He would have preferred to have stayed away, not because he was jealous nor through fear of being embarrassed, but because he believed that the meeting would be pointless and futile. It would change nothing, achieve nothing, mean nothing. But he had promised Suzanne that he would visit them and to give up a couple of hours was a small sacrifice, when he had so many empty evenings to spare.

Her lover was named Gaston. He was solidly built, slow in speech and movement, but good-natured. It did not seem to Gautier that the man was sly enough, persistent enough, or attractive enough to have stolen another man's wife. They shook hands and sat down to share a bottle of wine which Gaston opened, while Suzanne watched them as she dealt with the customers in the café, looking flustered but content.

'Do you miss your police days?' Gautier asked him.

'I never get time to. It's a hard life running a place like this. A lot of our trade comes early in the morning from people on their way to work and at night we keep open as long as there's anyone here. They stay to all hours sometimes, playing cards.'

'What made you choose this particular bistro?'

The question Gautier was really asking was why had they chosen that district. Suzanne's father, who had built up a successful business in the wholesale china trade, was not short of money and could easily have bought them a café on the Left Bank where the clientèle would have been drawn from students or lawyers or politicians.

'I was brought up here,' Gaston explained. 'And I began my time with the police in the eighteenth arrondissement, before they moved me to the fifteenth. Besides, Suzanne's father used to do business with this place and reckoned it was a little gold mine. It belonged to a policeman before we took it over and that helps in a district like Pigalle, I can tell you.'

Gautier could understand why that should be true. Since Haussmann, commissioned by the emperor to redevelop Paris, had pulled down the walls of the city forty years previously, the district around Place Pigalle had become progressively more disreputable. Before that time Montmartre had been a seedy village outside Paris and beyond the butte or hill of Montmartre there was the 'Maquis', where an unkempt collection of shanties and huts sheltered a tribe of cut-throats, apaches and rag-and-bone men who, by night, moved into Pigalle and Place Blanche to attack and rob passers-by and terrorize the shopkeepers. Not unnaturally they would keep clear of a café run by a former policeman, knowing that he was likely to have policemen friends who would protect him.

'Do you get much crime around here?' Gautier asked.

'Too much. The scum of the earth hang around the district. If you ever want to have an enemy removed, let me know. I could find you a dozen people who would do it for a hundred francs.'

As he was finishing what he was saying, Gaston began to look embarrassed, as though he had suddenly realized that he might be making a gaffe. My God, Gautier thought, he believes that I might think of him as an enemy, that I might want to have him assassinated. The idea was so preposterous that he wanted to laugh and if he had known Gaston better, he might have been able to share the humour of the situation with him.

Instead he said: 'Other people's killings are enough trouble, without setting up any of my own.'

'I suppose so, but even so life must be more interesting with the Sûreté than it ever was at the fifteenth.'

'That's true, certainly.'

'Is Commissaire Druot still in charge there?'

'Yes, but it's his last year. He retires in the autumn.'

They drifted into police talk, gossip about officers they had known, about promotions and disgraces, about spectacular crimes and others which had ended in fiasco. Like all neutral ground, it was safe with no danger of accidental wounding from stray remarks. Between the two of them they finished the bottle of wine.

By ten o'clock only half-a-dozen customers remained in the Café Soleil d'Or, four playing cards while the other two, a middle-aged couple, sat in a corner immersed in a long argument about the arrangements for the funeral of a deceased cousin. Since she was no longer being kept busy, Suzanne was able to join the two men, drawing up a chair to their table.

'I have a bottle of something special I'd like you to taste,' Gaston told Gautier, thinking evidently that their meeting was an occasion which ought to be celebrated.

While he was away fetching the special bottle, Suzanne said: 'I'm glad you like him, Jean-Paul,' and smiled gratefully, as though it was only out of the goodness of his heart that Gautier had consented to like Gaston.

'I'm sure the two of you will make a success of this place.'

'I believe we will. Perhaps I was never meant to just run a home.'

'Perhaps not.' Gautier knew that more than anything Suzanne would have liked to have had children and made a home for them.

Before they could get enmeshed further in this dangerous topic, Gaston returned with his bottle, which was old and dusty and contained an apricot liqueur. The bottle, he explained as he poured three generous glasses, was one of a batch which had been handed down to him by his great-grandfather.

The liqueur was strong and too sweet for his taste, but Gautier was obliged through courtesy to drink two glasses of it and when, eventually, he left the Café Soleil d'Or, he knew he was on the precarious ledge between sobriety and drunkenness. As he walked southwards towards the centre of the city, he thought about the evening he had just spent. Suzanne's motives in wanting him to meet Gaston were no doubt praiseworthy. In all probability she was trying to atone for the wrong which she believed she had done him, by offering him friendship and a relief from loneliness. If that had been her plan it had misfired. Now for the first time since she had left him, he felt alone.

His wife and her lover would soon be shutting up their café, after which they would sleep together. Although after ten years their marriage had no longer been a riot of passion, he missed the physical pleasures they had shared. While they had been together, he had enjoyed a mistress from time to time: Monique, the superstitious little dressmaker, and Claudine, the artist's model from Montmartre. Now, in a sudden and uncharacteristic mood of self-pity, he decided that no one wanted him except the ageing wife of a minister of France.

Thinking about sex reminded him of Clémentine. The displeasing scene in her apartment was still etched in his memory, but tonight the outlines were a little blurred by drink, the hurt of her scorn less sharp. He recalled, too, their meeting the previous day. She had made him promise that he would tell her as soon as he learnt anything about Monterant's death which would demolish the rumours the newspapers had been spreading and rescue Clémentine's fading popularity. By the next morning, it was true, she would be reading of Pelotti's confession in the papers, but there was still time for him to keep his promise.

A fiacre was standing at the next corner and climbing aboard it he told the driver to drive him to Rue de Courcelles. Clémentine had told him he would be welcome at any time, day or night, and he would keep her at her word. The drink which had clouded the memory of the evening when she had rebuffed him, had also made him indifferent to the possibility of another rebuff. He had kept one promise that evening to Suzanne, he told himself and now he would keep another.

The concierge admitted him to the building where Clémentine lived without question, either recognizing him from his previous visit or because she knew who he was. By this time every concierge and servant in the Plaine Monceau must be aware that he was the inspector from the Sûreté in charge of the investigations into Monterant's death. Upstairs Clémentine opened the door and did not appear surprised to see him.

All she said was: 'My maid has already retired.'

'You did say I could come at any time.'

'And I meant it. Does this mean you have good news for me at last?'

'Yes. A criminal named Pelotti has confessed to poisoning Sophie Monterant. He's the man who killed Lucie Bertron.'

Relief flooded into her face. The anxiety in her eyes was swept away, to be replaced with delight. 'Is this really true?'

'Yes. You'll be able to read all about it in *Le Matin* tomorrow without doubt.'

'I can't believe it.'

In spite of himself, Gautier was touched by her pleasure. 'Tomorrow evening your public, ashamed of the way they have treated you, will give you the greatest ovation you've ever received. You'll see.'

She looked at him searchingly. 'But you don't believe this Pelotti killed Monterant, do you, Jean-Paul?'

'There can be no doubt that he did. In his confession he described the poison that had been used and how it had been added to the chocolates.' Pelotti had appeared again in front of Judge Rolland and Gautier had seen a copy of the examination when he had returned to the Sûreté from the Salle Delacroix earlier that evening.

'Then what is worrying you?'

'I'd like to know why he killed her. Pelotti made his living off women. He says Monterant invited him to her bed and then refused to reward him.'

'That couldn't be true. Sophie only slept with men who could be of use to her. She was a cold fish, that one.'

'From what I've seen and heard of her, you're right.'

Gautier did not mention his other reason for disbelieving Pelotti's story. Earlier that day he had searched Sophie Monterant's diary and had been unable to find any reference to the Italian. Apart from 'Rimrod', 'Monge' and the unfortunate 'Brainemist', she did not appear to have made love with any men during the past month or so.

'Does it really matter why he poisoned her?'

'Probably not.'

They were standing facing each other in the drawing-room. She moved closer to him and smiled. He was surprised to see it was almost an exact replica of the smile Adèle Charvet had given him that afternoon, lascivious and suggestive. For one confused moment he wondered where he was and whether he was drunk or dreaming.

'Thank you for telling me about this man Pelotti. But was that all you had in mind when you came here tonight?'

'What else could there be?'

'This.'

Reaching up, she pulled his face down to hers and kissed him on the lips. Caution told him that he should not respond and he accepted the kiss passively. She looked at him, anxiously it seemed, and then kissed him again, her mouth eager and demanding. The effect of the wine he had been drinking still lingered and he felt his resolve weaken.

'That's what you came for, isn't it?' she whispered.

'Yes.' His voice sounded hoarse and unreal.

When they kissed again, she pressed her body against his. This time, he told himself, she would not, she could not turn back. Gently he caressed her shoulders and the back of her neck and then allowed his fingers to move slowly down her back. Then suddenly, abruptly, aware of his desire, she pulled her mouth away from his.

'No!'

'What's the matter?'

'Nothing.'

Though her face was turned away, her body was still close against his. A slow surge of frustration began to mount in him, driving him to a cold, controlled anger. Then she looked at him and he saw tears in her eyes. Anger would be futile. Gently he took a strand of hair which had fallen over her face and pushed it back into place.

'Can't you understand?' Her voice had the thin, harsh sound of despair. 'I can't give myself to you. I can't give myself to anyone.'

He smiled and said lightly: 'Do you want me to take you by force then?'

Without looking at him, the tears still glistening in her eyes, she nodded.

Much later they lay side by side in her bed, not touching each other but still close. She had struggled at first, kicking and swearing the obscenities of her urchin childhood, fighting not Gautier but her own desire. Then, suddenly, it had become a shared experience, frustration and loneliness swept aside by the flood of physical pleasure which they had found in each other, given each other.

Now Clémentine said, reflectively and without vanity: 'I didn't realize a man could ever want me like that.'

'Why not?'

'Because I'm not vain about my body, I suppose.'

Wishing to reassure her, Gautier reached out a caressing hand and his fingers touched her breasts. They were small but well-formed and firm. She took his hand and pressed it to her.

'I made my début as a singer,' she said, 'in a music hall in Lille.'

'Was it a success?'

'Hardly. I'll tell you about it.'

The story she told him began when, after two years in the theatre with little success, Clémentine had decided to become a caf'conc' singer. She had obtained an engagement in Lille, where she meant to try out her repertoire and some ideas for a new style of interpretation. But the audience at the music hall had conservative ideas about entertainment. They expected all female singers to be ample, big-busted women who would give them vulgar songs with suggestive winks and gestures. So when Clémentine appeared, slim and young and pale, they greeted her with derision. From up in the gallery some wag had called out: 'Ou sont ses tétons?—Where are her tits?' From another part of the house came an answering voice. 'She's left them in her trunk.'

Quickly the theme had been taken up with cruel delight by the audience, with one section chanting the question while another yelled the response. Clémentine's act was reduced to a fiasco. News travelled quickly in provincial towns and the next night the audience arrived prepared to give the singer from Paris the same ironical reception. Clémentine had been engaged to appear for three weeks, but after three nights the management paid her off and sent her home to Paris.

'I've lived with that humiliation for years,' Clémentine said when she finished the story. 'But do you know, I've never been able to tell anyone about it before.'

'Perhaps you've never found the right confessor.'

'No, it isn't that. Now that Sophie Monterant and her ghost have finally vanished, I'm a different person, a new woman.'

Raising himself up on to one elbow, Gautier looked at her. 'You must not believe that. The real truth is that now Monterant has gone, you are beginning to be your real self, to live your own life.'

'I don't follow you.'

'You wanted to emulate her in everything and mistakenly you tried to imitate her.'

'Me? Imitate her? That's crazy!'

'You tried to act like her, you took an apartment in the same district, you wanted to behave like she did, using people, becoming hard and aloof and calculating.'

'Don't be absurd! I hated her.'

'Love, hate, envy, admiration; they're just words. What you have never realized, my dear, is that you had no need to imitate Sophie. You have a greater talent than she had, you have a much more sympathetic character, you are a much more attractive woman, a more desirable woman.'

She did not protest nor argue but lay silent, thinking over what he had said. Looking at the outlines of her body, he found himself wondering how he had ever thought of her as thin and gaunt. That had been the impression she made on him when he had first seen her on the stage of L'Attentat, but he knew now that although she was small, her limbs were in perfect proportion to her body which, in spite of its slenderness, had a voluptuousness just as compelling as that of any of the ample nudes in the paintings on display at the Salle Delacroix that afternoon. He felt the slow arousing of desire once again.

'My God!' Clémentine suddenly exclaimed, wonderingly, 'you're right!'

'Do you mean I'm right when I say you imitated Sophie or when I say that you're desirable?'

'Am I desirable?'

'Do I have to use force again to prove it?'

'No.' Sitting up she pushed him back on to the bed and leaned over him. She said softly: 'This time it's you, my love, who is going to be ravished.'

17

WHILE THEY SLEPT, Gautier had a vivid dream. In the dream he was engulfed by a powerful scent which, although he could not smell it, he recognized as the perfume of Adèle Charvet. It swept over him in a mist that billowed down from distant hills covered in mimosa and brightly coloured flowers. In the middle of the mist stood his old schoolmaster, Monsieur Fénix, an enormous man with a huge, bulging head who, it was rumoured, had once been a wrestler in the court of an Algerian sultan. Monsieur Fénix was saying: 'Remember, my children, the greatest single capacity of the human mind is the power of logical thought.'

When he awoke a thin shaft of sunlight was piercing the soft darkness of the room through a crack in the shutters. He reached for his watch which lay on a table beside the bed and found that he could just make out the hands. Swearing mildly he swung his legs over the side of the bed and began searching for his clothes.

'What's the matter, my love?' Clémentine said drowsily.

'It's past ten o'clock.'

'So?'

'I should have been at work hours ago.'

'Have you forgotten that it's Sunday?'

He realized that she was right and the knowledge was unwelcome. He no longer looked forward to the slow, leisurely pleasures of Sunday. It had become a makeshift day of time spent on small tasks at home or wasted elsewhere, a day when self-discipline had to compete with boredom and was usually defeated. He climbed back into bed with Clémentine, glad to have an an excuse to postpone the act of rising and dressing and finding something to do.

'What kind of a man is General Lafitte?' The question had been hovering at the back of his mind.

'Sympathetic. I liked him.'

'Even after the way he treated you?'

'One cannot help feeling sorry for him. He just does not realize what a pathetic figure he presents. Do you know what he's most proud of, what he believes was his great achievement as Minister of War?'

'No, tell me.'

'He discovered that French army bands were playing no less than 179 different versions of the "Marseillaise". So he studied them all, selected what he considered was the best and made it the authorized version. All bands were forbidden by ministerial decree to play any other.'

'Not exactly the way to make a place for oneself in history!'

'He was a poor soldier and an even worse minister, but for all that he believes that the army is everything. He grows angry if his family and his friends forget to address him as "Mon Général".'

Clémentine had been lying on her back and now she rolled over and looked at Gautier. 'You arc still thinking about Sophie Monterant's death, aren't you?'

'Yes, I admit it. You can call it habit, a bad police habit.'

The murder in Rue Murillo was still in his thoughts but it was not merely through force of habit. He had still not been able to see a picture of the crime that satisfied him, a picture in which cause and effect and means and opportunity and motive fitted into place as they should do. Instead he was conscious of an unformed idea, elusive and imprecise, which nagged at his mind but would not take recognizable shape.

'Mon Général,' he said aloud thoughtfully. 'Could that be contracted to "Monge", I wonder.'

'What in the name of God are you talking about?'

'Do you by any chance have a piece of paper anywhere?'

'I suppose there would be some in the writing bureau.'

Gautier climbed out of the bed, drew a curtain and pushed one shutter back far enough to let in the light he needed. As Clémentine had said, there was paper in the bureau and a pencil and he sat down to work.

If Sophie Monterant had used a contraction of 'Mon Général' as her private name for Lafitte, then the other names he had found in her diary might have been devised in a similar way. He wrote out the name 'Rimrod' in capital letters and stared at it. For a long time he was puzzled and then suddenly he saw a possible answer. If one reversed the word one had 'Dormir'. He remembered the Comtesse de Limousin telling him that the comte had an incurable habit of falling asleep at all times and in unexpected places. Perhaps Sophie Monterant might have been provoked into giving the comte the name 'Rimrod' after he had fallen asleep during one of their more intimate evenings together.

He wrote out the remaining names which he remembered seeing in the actress's diary: 'Jockey', 'Labiste', 'Brainemist', 'Spumantisi'.

The name 'Jockey' had not featured in the diary in recent months, so he did not waste too much time over it, deciding that in all probability it was Sophie's way of referring to the President of the Jockey Club, whose name had been listed in her address book. 'Labiste' was less straightforward until suddenly he saw that it could be an anagram of the word 'bestial'. A name like that would have appealed to the actress's sardonic sense of humour.

While he was studying the two remaining names on the list he heard Clémentine laugh behind him. He turned his head to ask her: 'What is so amusing?'

'What are you doing naked at that desk? Composing passionate verses to some mistress?'

'Nothing so romantic, I fear.'

'In that case it should not interrupt your inspiration if I go and make us some coffee.'

'What about your maid? Will it matter if she finds me here?'

'You need have no fear. Your reputation is safe. I allow Marie-France to have Sundays to herself. She goes to mass in the morning and then straight from there to see her parents in Ivry.'

While Clémentine was out of the room making their breakfast, Gautier looked once more at the two names which he had not so far deciphered. When he had read Sophie Monterant's diary, he had supposed that one of the names might have been used for Henri Charvet and he began working first on 'Brainemist', writing the letters which made up the word in different sequences and combinations, looking for an anagram. It seemed meaningless. Then he found that by omitting two letters he had 'Ministre'. Finally he had the answer: Ministre BA.

This surely, he reasoned, must be intended to signify the Minister of Beaux-arts. Now he was left only with 'Spumantisi'. When he had first seen the name in the diary, he had supposed it to be of Italian origin. There was, he knew, an Italian wine called Spumante and he wondered whether Sophie Monterant had invented a diminutive of it, which she had used contemptuously for some lover who had not pleased her. Now he quickly realized that it was an anagram of 'Impuissant'.

The adjective, as he wrote it down, stirred in him a quickening anticipation. It was an emotive word, not to be lightly used, for to be described as impotent was the most wounding insult a Frenchman could receive. Duels in deadly earnest had been fought for less. He wondered briefly whether this might have been the name Monterant had used for Pelotti and that it would support the Italian's story of the night he had spent with the actress. Then he dismissed the idea. Pelotti's presence at the first performance of *La Dame aux Camélias* would scarcely have lent the occasion a cachet, particularly at a time when he was being hunted by the police for the murder of Lucie Bertron.

While he was thinking about the name, Clémentine came back into the bedroom carrying a tray with a jug of coffee, bread still warm from the oven and butter. She drew the curtains, opened the shutters, set the tray down on her dressing-table and poured the coffee. As he took a cup from her, Gautier noticed lying on the tray an envelope addressed to Clémentine, which had probably been brought up by the concierge with the morning bread. She took the envelope and placed it unopened into a drawer of the dressing-table.

'How are your literary efforts progressing?' she asked him.

'It isn't a poem, it's a puzzle.'

'What kind of puzzle?'

Gautier told her about the made-up names which Sophie Monterant had employed in her diary to describe lovers and intimate men friends. Then, showing her the sheet of paper on which he had been scribbling, he explained how, by manipulating words, the actress had concealed the real identity of the people to whom she had been referring. He showed her how he had been able to identify the Comte de Limousin, General Jacques Lafitte and the Minister of Beaux-arts.

'There is one name which intrigues me and which I can't seem to connect with any man in her life,' he concluded.

'Does it have to be another man?'

'What do you mean?'

'My mother always told me that the solution to any problem is usually the one you should have thought of first, the most obvious one. Why could Sophie not have used more than one name for a man? After all, she was writing for herself, so she would have known whom she meant.'

Cradling his coffee in his cupped hands, Gautier looked at her thoughtfully. He said slowly: 'Holy Virgin! I wonder if that is the answer.'

Just outside the Gare St Lazare, there was a barber who kept his shop open on Sundays. Gautier walked there from Clémentine's apartment and, as he sat in the chair, savoured the sensation of being shaved, the touch of hot towels and the smell of pomade and brilliantine. The enterprising barber, whose gleaming bald pate did not prevent him from selling hundreds of bottles of his own hair restorer, was also a man of discernment and, recognizing that he had a customer with a problem on his mind, he said nothing as he manipulated the razor. So Gautier was also able to enjoy the luxury of time to think.

What Clémentine had said to him over breakfast, inconsequential enough in itself, had struck an unexpected response in his mind, recalling a whole string of half-forgotten incidents and impressions: Sophie Monterant celebrating her theatrical triumph with a chocolate, the concierge's evasiveness when Gautier had first questioned her, Gaston's opinion of the criminals who hung around the district near the Café Soleil d'Or. Linked together they had given him an idea, but it was no more than an idea and there was much to be explained, much to be done before he could fashion the idea into a plausible theory of why Sophie Monterant had died.

From the barber's shop he went to Rue Murillo. The concierge at Monterant's house was not in her lodge but away at morning mass. Her husband whom she had left to deputize for her, an old man with no teeth but sharp, inquisitive eyes, told Gautier that Françoise was not in the building either, nor could he say when she might return. The maid, it appeared, had left the previous evening to visit the home of the family with whom she was to start work at the beginning of the following month. She was to be shown round the house, meet the other servants and have her duties explained to her. Surprisingly she had not yet returned to Rue Murillo, although there had been no talk of her spending the night with her new employers.

Telling the concierge's husband that he would be back later, Gautier went next to Sûreté headquarters. There were facts he could be checking while he waited to question Françoise and an outline of a plan was forming in his mind. When the policeman standing guard outside the entrance to the Sûreté told him Lemaire was the inspector on duty that Sunday, the plan took final shape.

The duty inspector's office was on the ground floor and he found Lemaire compiling a log of the day's robberies, assaults and killings and the action that had been taken in each case. Lemaire was good at desk work for he had an orderly and unadventurous mind. There were times when Gautier envied him.

'I didn't expect to see you here today, Jean-Paul,' he told Gautier.

'There are still some aspects of the Monterant affair which don't satisfy me.'

'Loose ends you wish to tie up?'

'One might put it that way.'

'You always were a conscientious devil. How can I help?'

Gautier told him that when he had collected Pelotti at the Gare de Lyon, the inspector escorting the prisoner back from the Italian border had handed him a brown-paper package. According to Pelotti the package had contained not only money, but something that would cause an explosion in Paris.

'That's right,' Lemaire replied. 'Pelotti has boasted to me more than once about his precious package. He said it contained his insurance.'

'But you never saw what was in it?'

149

'No. Courtrand keeps the package locked up and I've never even been allowed to handle it.'

'Hasn't the juge d'instruction ever referred to it during the examination?'

'Never. Rolland made it clear from the start that he was not interested in any of Pelotti's earlier crimes or other activities, nor in his private life unless it was categorically related to Lucie Bertron's murder.'

'But surely things changed when Pelotti admitted to killing Monterant?'

'Well, all I can say is that the package or its contents have never been mentioned in the official interrogations.'

What Lemaire was saying only strengthened Gautier's suspicions that there were aspects in the Pelotti affair which were being deliberately concealed by people in authority. He told Lemaire: 'I wish to find out what the package holds.'

'That's impossible. As I told you, Courtrand keeps it locked up in his safe.'

'As duty inspector you have the key to his office and to the safe.'

Lemaire was horrified. 'Do you know what you're asking, Jean-Paul?'

'I'm only asking you to turn your back while I borrow the keys. You'll have them back in ten minutes and nothing in the safe will be removed, I can promise you that.'

Lemaire hesitated and then shrugged his shoulders. 'All right. I owe you a favour. Take the keys and you can take your time, too. Courtrand isn't in Paris but at his home in the country.'

Taking the keys, Gautier went upstairs to Courtrand's office. The safe was a small, elegant model which had been put on the market by an enterprising manufacturer a year or two previously as being ideal for a lady's boudoir, but which any self-respecting thief would have been able to open in under two minutes. Having a safe in his office at all was just another of the director's many affectations, since there were plenty of facilities in the Sûreté for keeping important papers secure.

Pelotti's parcel stood alone on the upper shelf of the safe, like a rare and highly prized sausage on the counter of a charcuterie.

It was no longer sealed, but loosely tied with string. When he opened it Gautier found a neat bundle of brown envelopes to the top one of which had been attached a police message form. The message read:

To: The Director-General, the Sûreté.
From: Inspector Dubois, Border Police.
Message: Acting on your instructions I boarded the night train from Paris to Milan and apprehended the prisoner, Marcel Pelotti. Among his possessions I found the enclosed papers which I am packaging and sending to you under seal.

Gautier began to open the envelopes, which were all unsealed and he soon understood why Pelotti had described them as his insurance, for each of them contained a selection of incriminating articles and a carefully compiled dossier of information which would be worth a sizeable fortune to a skilled blackmailer.

The first envelope referred to a certain Madame Antoinette Bize of Neuilly, whose husband, according to Pelotti's notes, was the director of a substantial trading company with interests in France's colonies and in the Far East. Madame Bize was clearly not only indiscreet but a sentimental lady and the envelope contained not only a bundle of passionate letters which she had written to Pelotti six years previously, but a lock of her hair, now dry and faded.

The material in the second envelope had been unwittingly provided by a spinster, the thirty-year-old niece of the Archbishop of Paris. Since she had evidently been too prudent to put pen to paper or scissors to her hair, Pelotti had contrived a different form of proof of their past affair. In the absence of her parents, the lady had admitted him to her bedroom and he had written out an exact and detailed description of the room and its furnishings and the time and day of the seduction. As a final touch to dispel any possible doubts about his claims, he had added a note to the effect that the lady had a crescent-shaped birthmark on the left side of her stomach.

There were nine envelopes in the bundle, arranged as Gautier discovered in the chronological order of Pelotti's amours. He found what he was looking for in the last envelope, for it had been in the first few months of the present year that the Italian had been Adèle Charvet's lover. She had written him not romantic letters but a number of brief, imperious notes. The first one which Gautier read was typical of all the others.

Monsieur,
   I look forward to meeting you tomorrow at 1600 hours in the Hôtel Printemps in Rue François 1er. A reservation has been made in the name of Madame Challot. I count on your being there and on your discretion.
                                             Adèle

The later notes were slightly less impersonal, slightly more urgent in tone, but the style and the content and the chosen meeting places were always the same. The Hôtel Printemps was, as Gautier knew, an exceedingly discreet and expensive hôtel de rendezvous where rooms were available by the afternoon and which was widely used by society ladies for assignations with their lovers.

On at least one occasion, Madame Charvet's good sense and caution had failed her, for attached to the notes was a photograph of herself. It was a studio portrait, when she was in her thirties and still retained a certain youthful loveliness. She had been photographed with her shoulders bare and her hair in tight curls, staring into space with an ethereal wistfulness, a daring pose for a respectable married lady and one which was intended to be seductive. Written across the bottom of the photograph in a bold, decisive hand were the words: 'To Marcel, with fervent memories of the hours we spent together. Adèle.'

As he replaced the letters and photographs in their envelopes, Gautier wondered what it was about Pelotti that had provoked mature, respectable women into such appalling indiscretions. Was it that they knew their husbands would in the end have to pay for their recklessness and was this, as Adèle Charvet had suggested, their revenge for past wrongs?

18

THAT AFTERNOON Gautier returned to Clémentine's apartment. He had been first to Rue Murillo where the concierge, now back in her quarters, had no more news of Françoise. She did not know the address of the house in which the old servant would soon be starting work, but she had reminded him that it had been Mademoiselle Lyse who had found her the place.

When Clémentine opened the door to his knock, she appeared surprised and a little confused to see him. They had made no arrangement to meet again when he had left her at mid-day, although he had felt there was an unspoken understanding between them that he should return and soon.

He told her what he wished to know and she smiled as she replied: 'So, you are still chasing the answer to your riddles?'

'Yes, but the chase is almost over.'

'Françoise is going to work for a Madame Desbordes. Her husband is a professor at the Sorbonne and they live in Rue Saint-Jacques. It's a big old-fashioned house at number nineteen, I believe. They are a good family, pious and charitable, who will look after Françoise well and see she does not starve in her old age.'

Before he left, Gautier paused at the door and said: 'After I have spoken with Françoise, would you wish me to come back?'

'Not tonight,' she replied and then as though to soften the abruptness of her reply, she reached out to touch his arm and added: 'Last night was wonderful, chéri! But you taught me much about myself and now I need time to think. We'll make love again soon.'

As he went downstairs to the fiacre which he had kept waiting outside the house, Gautier wondered whether he was disappointed or not by her reply. In one way he had been looking forward to spending a second night with Clémentine, to her company as well as to sensual pleasures, to the reassuring sensation which he had almost forgotten of waking from sleep with someone lying close beside him. At the same time his innate reserve and caution made him reluctant to form new attachments and new habits.

As the fiacre carried him southwards and then across the Seine towards Rue Saint-Jacques, he put Clémentine out of his mind. Instead he wondered, with mounting uneasiness, what might have happened to Françoise. There were a number of plausible and simple explanations of why she should not have returned to Rue Murillo, but for her to disappear at the precise time when he needed to talk with her and when only she could confirm the theory he had been forming about her mistress's death, was a disturbing coincidence.

A manservant opened the door of number nineteen, Rue Saint-Jacques, and took Gautier in to see the master and mistress of the house. Professor and Madame Desbordes were, as Clémentine had said, a solid, virtuous bourgeois couple. He was tall and round-shouldered, as though bent under the weight of his learning, she motherly and dutiful.

After introducing himself, Gautier said to them: 'Excuse me for disturbing you, Professor, and you, Madame, at this hour on a Sunday afternoon.'

'We were expecting someone from the police,' the professor replied, 'but I had not supposed it would be a matter for the Sûreté.'

'You say you were expecting the police!' Gautier exclaimed. 'May I ask why?'

'I sent our manservant round to the local commissariat this morning to report the matter.'

'What matter?'

'A most serious case of assault. Last night as she was leaving our house, Françoise Bonnot, who is to be our maid, was brutally beaten up and left for dead.'

'But she is not dead?'

'No. By a miracle she survived, but her life is still in danger.'

154

'Where is she?'

'Upstairs. We had her brought into our home and our family physician came at once to tend her. He returned a short time ago and is with Françoise now.'

'It is not known who attacked her, I suppose?'

The professor shook his head. 'Unfortunately, no. Two men were seen running away. One supposes they were prowling in the neighbourhood, looking for someone to attack and rob.'

'It is not what one expects in this district.'

'No,' the professor agreed. 'Footpads and criminals would not consider academics and students worth robbing.'

'I would like to speak to Françoise,' Gautier said.

'I cannot say whether she is well enough, Monsieur l'Inspecteur. Perhaps you should consult the doctor who is with Françoise even now. Our manservant, Claude, will conduct you to her room while we wait here.'

Gautier followed the manservant to a bedroom on the second floor of the house, which was clearly not one of the servants' rooms but had been that of the eldest son of the family, who was away from home doing his military service.

Françoise was lying in the bed, pale and motionless, with her head heavily bandaged as the doctor, who had just finished his examination, was replacing his instruments in his bag. Gautier took him on one side and quickly explained the purpose of his visit.

'I doubt whether the poor woman will be able to assist you, Inspector,' the doctor said. 'She has been partly paralysed by the terrible beating those voyous inflicted on her and she seems to have lost her power of speech, for the time being at least.'

'But she is still conscious?'

'Yes. But she is an old woman. To be frank I believe that her chances of surviving this ordeal are small.'

'Have I your consent to try and question her?'

'By all means, if you think she will understand.'

Taking a chair which stood in a corner of the room, Gautier placed it by the bed and sat down. Françoise opened her eyes and stared at him. Her face bore the look of a frightened animal, captive and alert to danger but helpless.

'I need your help again, Françoise,' Gautier said gently. 'If we are to find the people who attacked you and those who murdered your mistress, it is most important that you should try to answer my questions.'

The maid's face twitched, as though she were trying to speak, but no sound came. She looked appealingly towards the doctor.

'I know you cannot speak, Françoise, but don't let that worry you. What we will do is this. I am going to suggest certain things to you and if what I say is correct, just blink your eyes once. If I am wrong, blink twice. Do you think you can manage that?'

Françoise hesitated and then, with an obvious effort, blinked once. Gautier said 'Excellent! We will begin. Now we know that before you came to Paris, your home was in Grasse in the Alpes Maritimes, where they make essences for perfumes. The town is famous for it. We also know that the family of the Minister of Beaux-arts, Monsieur Charvet, were in the perfume business and also lived in the South. I believe it is possible that you knew Henri Charvet and his family at that time.'

The maid blinked her eyes once so Gautier continued: 'Did you work for his family, by any chance?' The question was met with two blinks, so he tried again: 'Perhaps you worked for friends or neighbours of the family?'

Another single blink showed Gautier he was moving in the right direction and, encouraged, he continued his probing. 'In her diary your mistress wrote that you disapproved of Monsieur Charvet and you seemed determined to stop him from becoming too friendly with her. This must have been because of something you knew about him; something discreditable from the days back in Grasse.' Françoise blinked once and he went on: 'Perhaps it was something he had done as a young man, something disgraceful. Ah, I see that my guess is correct. What could it have been, I wonder, that makes you despise Monsieur Charvet so. Was it something that harmed you personally? Was it to do with money? Were the police involved?'

A succession of double blinks came as Françoise's reply to his questions. Determined to discover what Françoise knew, Gautier put his imagination to work, trying to picture what a young man brought up in an affluent, respectable family might have done to earn the scorn and hatred of a country servant. The classic way for a boy of good family to misbehave was by giving a local girl a child, but this was common enough in the country not to provoke more than a few disapproving sniffs and a lecture from the curé. A country servant would have been accustomed to that kind of youthful folly and would certainly not have carried a grudge against Henri Charvet for thirty years or more on that account. Françoise had been protective towards Sophie Monterant, and if she had tried to send Charvet packing, it must have been because she was afraid that he would either hurt her mistress or damage her reputation.

'I'm trying to imagine what the minister could have done that turned you against him, Françoise. Did it cause a local scandal? No? That might have been, of course, because his family used their money and influence to hush it up.' Gautier saw from her expression that he was right on this last point. He went on: 'Would I be able to find out about this business from his family or from people in the neighbourhood. There must have been another party involved?'

The doctor had been standing behind Gautier as he questioned Françoise and now he spoke. 'She appears to be trying to tell you something.'

Françoise's mouth was twitching and her jaw moved almost imperceptibly up and down, as she struggled to speak. A faint sound, not unlike the rustle of dried leaves stirred by a light breeze, came from her lips. He leaned forward over her until his ear was no more than a few centimetres from her face.

'What is it, Françoise?'

For several seconds her mouth kept twitching without making any identifiable sound. Then with a supreme effort she managed to whisper four words.

'They are all dead!'

Her eyes closed and her whole face appeared to sag with exhaustion. She seemed to be drifting into sleep when suddenly her body was shaken with a convulsion. Her face was distorted with a grimace of agony and her breathing turned into great, shuddering gasps as she fought for air. The doctor stepped forward quickly to help her but it was too late. For a few seconds, instinctively, she struggled for life and then her head fell back, the eyes staring into space.

'She can tell you no more, Monsieur,' the doctor said simply as he closed her eyes.

19

WITH HIS ELBOWS resting on the parapet of the wall that separated Quai Voltaire from the Seine, Gautier stared at the river as it flowed lazily by in the evening sunlight. The people of Paris were returning to their city, reluctantly, because their summer Sunday, spent in the fields or on the banks of the river in the country, eating, drinking, dancing, making love or just sleeping, was over. Two couples, the men in knickerbockers, the ladies in bouffant cycling bloomers, bicycled along the quai behind Gautier. Cycling had become fashionable in Paris, but in a country where for centuries the only sports ever practised were equestrianism and fencing, it was still regarded as eccentric and the sight of a cyclist was enough to provoke stares and sometimes a ribald cheer. When the black-bearded Dr Mardrus, translator of *A Thousand and One Nights*, and the young poetess, Lucie Delarue, arrived at the church of St Roch for their wedding in cycling attire, it caused a sensation.

Gautier did not even notice the cyclists, for his mind was fully occupied with what he sensed was for him the final problem of the Monterant affair. It was a problem requiring his decision and his alone, a choice of alternatives. He had reached a conclusion on why Sophie Monterant had died and the proper course of action now was for him to write a report setting out that conclusion and the evidence to support it, for his superior, the Director-General of the Sûreté. Courtrand would then decide what action should be taken.

What concerned him was that he had reached his conclusion by speculation and deduction and had little material proof to offer. He was afraid that Courtrand might, in his usual autocratic manner, dismiss the theory out of hand and even forbid Gautier to make any further enquiries. He knew, moreover, that he could not mention one of the links in the chain of his deductions without revealing that he had opened Courtrand's private safe.

The alternative was to ignore protocol and force the whole issue out into the open. It was a tactic he had used before, but a risky one and after the warning that Courtrand had already given him, he had no illusions about what might happen to him if he failed.

Facing him across the Seine were the headquarters of the Sûreté. It was the sight of the building in which he had so often been frustrated by officialdom and regulations, which finally decided him. Turning his back on it and on the river, he set out for Rue de Grenelle.

When he arrived at the residence of the Minister of Beaux-arts, an automobile was pulling up outside the house. It was the latest Panhard-Levassor, beautifully appointed, with highly polished woodwork, leather seats and brass headlamps, a model much coveted by wealthy Parisians who could afford expensive playthings. A chauffeur in a cream overall, brown leather leggings, a cream cap and goggles climbed down and helped first the minister and then Madame Charvet out of the car.

'Why, Inspector!' Charvet called out when he saw Gautier, 'have you been waiting for us? We've been for a drive in the country.'

Adèle Charvet held out her hand to Gautier. He could not be sure whether she was surprised to see him, for she was wearing a veil of the type used by ladies who were daring enough to ride in automobiles, which had been drawn down from above her hat and tied under her chin, covering her whole face.

'What do you think of my new automobile?' Charvet asked, pointing at the machine. 'It's the same model as that which won the road race to Lyon. Who but the French would have had the ingenuity to think of placing the engine at the front, where if it breaks down it is easily accessible?'

'The inspector did not come here on a Sunday evening to admire your car,' his wife said.

'No, Madame. I came to find out if it would be possible for me to have a few words with the minister.'

Charvet took Gautier's arm and squeezed it. 'Of course, of course. How could I refuse you anything after your heroism of yesterday?'

Still holding his arm, he led Gautier into the house behind Madame Charvet. A footman who had been holding the door open for them took the minister's hat and cane.

'I'll take the inspector to my study, Adèle,' Charvet called out to his wife who was removing her veil and hat as she went upstairs.

The study was smaller than that of the Comte de Limousin, its furnishings less artistically chosen or costly. The bourgeois and homely surroundings did not, however, prevent Charvet from observing the protocol of society and leaving Gautier to stand as he sat himself down at his desk.

'I regret, Monsieur le Ministre,' Gautier decided that formality deserved no less than formality in return, 'that I have bad news about the woman Françoise Bonnot.'

'Bonnot?'

'She is the maid of your former friend, Sophie Monterant.'

Gautier deliberately used the word 'amie', which to most Frenchmen would mean 'mistress', but Charvet chose to ignore the impertinence. He said pompously: 'And what is this news which you presume would be of interest to me?'

'Françoise was violently assaulted yesterday evening and left for dead.'

'Left for dead?'

'Yes, Monsieur le Ministre.'

'But that's terrible!'

'Fortunately the family of a nearby house took her in and sent for their physician to look after her.'

'Where did this take place?'

'In Rue Saint-Jacques.'

Charvet opened a silver cigar box, took out a cigar, cut it carefully and lit it. His manner was one of patient courtesy, as though having agreed to see Gautier he was prepared to hear him out, no matter how trivial the subject he had come to talk about. Gautier noticed that lying on the desk was a copy of a book recently published on the history of the official buildings of Paris and it was open at the chapter which dealt with the Elysée Palace. The minister, he decided, must be confident that the highest office in the republic would soon be his.

'These attacks on innocent wayfarers are becoming intolerable,' Charvet said. 'She was robbed, I suppose?'

'No criminal would make the mistake of trying to rob an old servant woman.'

'Then what was the reason for the attack?'

'The same reason why a box of poisoned chocolates was delivered at the home of Sophie Monterant.'

'What are you saying, man?' Charvet protested. 'That villain Pelotti has admitted to poisoning Madame Monterant.'

'He has admitted arranging for poison to be put in the chocolates and then taking them to her home.'

'Well?'

'They were not intended to kill Monterant. They were meant for Françoise.'

Charvet stopped gesticulating with his cigar as he had been doing or shrugging his shoulders or raising his bushy, white eyebrows. Suddenly he was still, very still and watchful.

'How do you know this?' he asked.

'It was a very clever plan,' Gautier replied, ignoring the direct question. 'The box of chocolates was addressed to Monterant, so if her maid ate one and died, everyone would assume she had been murdered by mistake and that the intended victim was Monterant.'

'But why should Françoise eat one of the chocolates sent to her mistress?'

'Because Monterant was worried that she was losing her figure. She had not eaten a chocolate or a bon-bon for more than a month.'

Charvet made a disparaging noise. 'And how could Pelotti possibly have known that?'

'Pelotti knew nothing and cared nothing. Like the two voyous who assaulted Françoise last night, he was only doing what he had been paid to do.'

'And who would pay to have a servant, an ignorant country-woman, killed?'

Gautier realized that Charvet, although he might be an astute politician, was too naïve to play the dangerous game of criminal deceit. A cleverer man would have told Gautier sharply that he was in no way concerned with the death of an actress's servant and brought the interview to an abrupt end. Instead Charvet sat before his desk, as though confronted by Mesmer himself, unable to do anything except listen. Knowing that he was the master now, Gautier drew up a chair and sat down facing him.

'The story begins many years ago,' he said, 'when Françoise was in service in the country not far from where she was born, near Grasse to be precise. There was a family in the neighbourhood, well-to-do people in the perfume business, who had a son, a young man perhaps not much more than an adolescent. Young men of good families are often a little wild, one might almost say it is expected of them. But this particular boy went too far. He behaved in a way that might have brought his family permanent disgrace, perhaps even trouble with the authorities, and it was only the money and local influence of his parents that saved him from the consequences of his act and prevented a scandal.'

Charvet's expression, the horror of a man confronted with the half-forgotten but fearful spectre of his own guilt, told Gautier that his stratagem was working. He had been choosing his words carefully, trying to conceal from Charvet how little he really knew about the incident which had made such a lasting impression on Françoise and which had so disgusted her. Then, even as he was speaking, an image from the previous day transposed itself on to his memory, a picture of the look on Charvet's face at the Salle Delacroix when he had been speaking to his secretary from the ministry, the effeminate Preule. He also remembered other things. Monterant's contemptuous reference in her diary to 'Brainemist' as a lover and why she had decided to give him the new name of 'Spumantisi'; how Charvet had squeezed his own arm outside the house a few minutes earlier; the remarks of the elderly deputy from Seine-et-Marne in the Café Corneille.

'Françoise was so shocked by the behaviour of this young man,' he went on, 'that she was reluctant to talk about it even now after all these years. But we can use our imagination and make a reasonable assumption. Could it not have been that he gave way to his unnatural passions, that he seduced another boy, someone much younger, the son of a neighbour, perhaps?'

Charvet's whole face seemed slowly to sag, as though flesh, muscles and bone were starting to disintegrate. Completely confident now, Gautier continued: 'The boy's family were bought off, one supposes, and that might well have seemed to be the end of the business. The young man leaves Grasse, comes to live in Paris and in due course enters politics. The past is forgotten and anyway who would bother about what a boy might have done thirty years ago? And then, unexpectedly, our politician finds that he is a candidate for the most important office that France has to offer. Now we have a totally different situation. No hint of scandal, however distant, must taint the office of President of the Republic, above all the scandal of pederasty. Our politician is respectably married, hard-working, of the highest integrity. If anyone has any doubts at all about him, it can only be because he shows so little interest in women. In France that alone could be enough to make people raise their eyebrows, ask questions. So he decides he must put these suspicions at rest by creating for himself a reputation for being, in a discreet way, a ladies' man, in other words a good Frenchman. What better way of doing this for a Minister of Beaux-arts than by paying excessive attentions to a beautiful and popular young actress?'

Through force of habit Gautier paused, waiting for a denial from the accused. Then collecting himself hurriedly, he continued. The last thing he wanted was to give Charvet an opportunity to temporize, to think.

'As a friend of mine would say, our politician needed to flaunt a woman before the public, like a flower in his buttonhole. It did not have to be a serious affair. But in selecting Sophie Monterant for this doubtful honour, he chose badly, for whom should he meet in her home but Françoise, the servant of the family whose son he had seduced, a ghost from the past he wished to forget. Françoise had a good memory. She had not forgotten the past and she was loyal and protective towards her mistress. She was not going to allow Monterant to make a fool of herself by unwittingly taking a pédé to her bed and she told our politician so. Can you imagine what a devastating shock it was to him?'

Charvet's head was bowed as though heavy with despair. Gautier could not resist a little delicate irony and he said: 'Ah, I can see

164

you can, Minister. Of course our politician's affair with Monterant was of no real consequence. He could have given her up and found another actress. But what about Françoise? She had not told her mistress what she knew, but could he ever be certain that she would always keep silent? What would she do when she learned that he was to become President of France? If she felt the same loyalty to her country as she did to her mistress, she might feel impelled to tell people about the past and his career would be destroyed.'

A bee which found its way into the room was trying to escape back into the evening sunshine. The noise it made thumping against the window-pane distracted Gautier's attention. He saw that the window overlooked a long, narrow garden at the back of the house and at the bottom of the garden there was a small pavilion, built on the model of a classical temple with Ionic pillars. It would have been a better place, he thought, for Adèle Charvet to entertain her lovers than an hôtel de rendezvous.

'You had no idea what to do,' he told Charvet, unconsciously dropping the pretence that he was recounting the story of an imaginary character. 'And then, by sheer chance you were presented with a solution to your dilemma. Your wife had been having an affair with Pelotti. You didn't mind that because you had always accepted that she would have to look elsewhere for the pleasures of the bed. Then Pelotti killed Lucie Bertron and was being hunted by the police. You offered him money; enough money to leave France and live in comfort for the rest of his days. All he had to do was put poison in some chocolates and deliver the box to Sophie Monterant's home. He probably never even knew they were intended for the maid.'

'What a preposterous accusation!' Charvet exclaimed. He was beginning to reassemble the fragments of his sangfroid and soon his mind, like the imprisoned bee, would be busily searching for a way of escaping from Gautier's accusations.

'Your mistake, Minister, was in trying to be clever. If in the first place you had paid a couple of cut-throats to kill Françoise, as you did in a panic yesterday, they could have taken their time and made a good job of it. No one would have guessed why she was being murdered and for what reason. How could they?'

'You're a courageous man, Inspector, to accuse a Minister of State in this way. One hopes for the sake of your future career that you have evidence to support these charges.'

'There's evidence enough.'

'The story of a servant? She has already accused one other person of murdering her mistress. Who is going to believe what—'

Before he could complete the sentence, the door of the study was thrown open. Adèle Charvet stood in the doorway and Gautier realized that she must have been outside listening to their conversation. 'Say nothing more, Henri,' she ordered her husband. 'The man is only trying to trap you. He has no evidence for anything he has said. The maid Françoise is dead.'

'Dead? Are you certain?'

'You're guessing, Madame,' Gautier said to her.

'Not at all. You have forgotten that wonderful invention, the telephone. I have just spoken to the Commissariat of Police for the sixteenth arrondissement. Françoise's death has been officially reported.'

'We do not have to rely on her evidence.'

'Are you saying that Marcel Pelotti would accuse my husband?' Adèle Charvet laughed scornfully. 'Evidently you don't know what type of man he is.'

Charvet rose from his chair, went round to the other side of the desk and stood next to his wife, linking his arm with hers. In spite of the many differences between their characters and inclinations, he appeared to find strength in her presence.

'Pelotti's bank can testify that he received a large sum of money shortly before he tried to leave Paris,' Gautier said. 'On the facts that we know, it could only have come from you, Monsieur Charvet.'

'Not necessarily.' Although she may have been taunting him, Adèle Charvet spoke quite seriously. 'Why should it not have been me?'

20

THE FOLLOWING MORNING an official visit to Paris by the Shah of Persia was due to begin. The French enjoyed entertaining foreign potentates and the spectacles which were arranged in their honour: a gala performance at the Opéra, firework displays, a banquet at the Elysée Palace. The visit meant special duty for large numbers of the Paris police, who would be stationed among the crowds which lined the streets as the imperial visitor drove through the city with a cavalry escort.

Another result of this particular visit was that the Director-General of the Sûreté arrived at headquarters much earlier than he normally did, not through any concern for the security of the shah, but because he had been invited to the reception which was the first event of the visit and he wished to finish his routine work for the day before he left for the Hôtel de Ville.

So it was that soon after nine o'clock he was reading the brief report which Gautier had written the previous night and which described the fatal attack on Françoise and Gautier's subsequent confrontation with the Minister of Beaux-arts. Gautier had handed him the report without explanation or preamble, for experience had taught him that any attempt to prepare Courtrand for unpalatable news only made his reception of it even more ill-tempered than usual.

To his surprise, what the Director-General read did not produce the explosive response he had expected. Instead as he put down the report Courtrand said thoughtfully: 'I have to say, Gautier, that I never believed Pelotti's explanation of why he should have wished to kill Monterant.'

'Are you saying that you believe the Minister of Beaux-arts was responsible?' Gautier asked him bluntly.

'What I believe is not important. Your interpretation of the facts is plausible; one might even say it is the only convincing explanation of otherwise inexplicable happenings. But how much of the most serious charge you are making can be proved?'

'Charvet made no attempt whatsoever to deny what I put to him. It was quite obvious from his whole manner that he is implicated not only in the poisoning of Monterant but in the death of Françoise. If his wife had not intervened I believe he might even have confessed.'

'Possibly, but will he admit anything if we take him before the juge d'instruction?'

'In my opinion definitely not.'

'Then we must ask ourselves what proof do we have firstly that the minister paid Pelotti to poison the chocolates and secondly that he hired men to batter the maid to death.'

Courtrand's question did not come as a surprise to Gautier, for he had been searching for an answer to it during much of the night just past. Now that Françoise was dead, it appeared that the only possibility of linking Charvet with the poisoning of Monterant was if Pelotti implicated him. He told Courtrand so.

'And do you consider that Pelotti might?'

'From what I saw of him, I would say not.'

'I agree. Pelotti is going to be guillotined in any case for killing Bertron, so what does he stand to gain by pleading that he was paid to poison Monterant?'

Gautier did not even suggest that Charvet might be incriminated by the two men who killed Françoise. He knew the way the Paris underworld worked. The men would certainly have come from another part of Paris and so not be recognized by anyone who saw them in the sixteenth arrondissement either before or after the attack on Françoise. They might even have been brought in from Marseille for the assignment and already be on their way back to lose themselves in that city's festering slums. Moreover the money they received would have been handed over to them by an intermediary and they would not even have known whom they were serving.

'Besides,' Courtrand continued, 'Pelotti has a curious belief that he must behave like a man of honour. He would never betray a confederate.'

'Why should he feel any obligation to Charvet?'

'Was it Charvet who actually paid him to poison the chocolates? Might it not have been, as she herself has suggested, Madame Charvet who approached him, when he was in trouble after killing Bertron, and offered him money to help him leave France, at the same time asking him to do her one last small favour?'

'Because she knew Françoise was in a position to ruin Charvet's career?'

'Precisely. From what I've heard, that lady is even more determined than Charvet that he should become President of the Republic.'

That might well be true, Gautier thought cynically. The first lady of France could reasonably expect to enjoy the same private freedom as certain presidents in the past whose scandalous love affairs had remained concealed from public eyes behind the closed doors of the Elysée Palace.

'I should have listened to Surat,' he told Courtrand. 'He told me poison was a woman's weapon.'

'The problem is what is to be done now.' Courtrand was evidently not in a mood to philosophize on the art of murder. 'What exactly do we have in the way of evidence against Charvet? An entry in a dead woman's diary where even his name is disguised, a concierge's identification, the knowledge that Pelotti mysteriously acquired a very considerable sum of money, and the whispered words of a dying servant?'

'That is about all.'

'Not very convincing, is it?' Courtrand asked sarcastically and then added: 'You realize, of course, Gautier, that you should have come to see me before you began to accuse the minister?'

'I was hoping to extract a confession from him.'

'We could have done that more easily if we could have invited him here to headquarters and faced him alone, away from his wife.'

Preferring to accept the rebuke rather than give the real reason why he had gone to Charvet's home the previous evening, Gautier was silent. Courtrand may have divined what was in his thoughts because he continued: 'You don't deceive me, Gautier. The real reason why you chose not to report this matter to me was that you thought I would take no action.'

'Monsieur Charvet is a minister of the government,' Gautier replied. 'In France people of such eminence appear to be above the law.'

'That isn't true!' Courtrand shouted angrily. 'You and some of your colleagues in this building believe that, because I treat important people with tact and consideration, I am in their pockets.'

'It is not you we blame, but official policy.'

'What you seem unable to comprehend,' Courtrand ranted on, ignoring his comment, 'is that people in important positions, those who serve the republic, are entitled to consideration and to their privacy. I regard it as my duty to see that they are not pestered nor spied upon nor abused over matters of no consequence. They suffer enough at the hands of the newspapers and the scandal-mongers without being assailed by the Sûreté as well. But when it comes to a criminal offence, no one—not even the highest in the land—is above the law and they never will be as long as I am Director-General of the Sûreté!'

It was not by any means the first time that Courtrand had lost his temper in the presence of Gautier, for he was a man whose pride or vanity were easily offended, but this time his anger did not appear to be that of a man stung by some trivial irritation or impertinence; it had the ring of a passion. If I did not know the man better, Gautier thought cynically, I might believe he means what he is saying.

'You have created this situation,' Courtrand said, 'through your conceit and your belief that you could handle the matter better on your own. Now I am left with only one course open to me. This morning Pelotti is due to appear before the juge d'instruction for a final examination. I will speak to Judge Rolland beforehand and if he agrees we will confront Pelotti with the accusation that he was paid for his part in the Monterant affair by Charvet.'

'And if he denies it?'

'Then, Gautier, you can reflect that you have been responsible for a miscarriage of justice.'

'Pelotti may be more inclined to implicate Charvet if he knows that he was betrayed.'

'Betrayed? What do you mean?'

170

'Somebody warned you that he would be on the night train to Milan.'

Courtrand looked at him sharply. He was obviously wondering how Gautier knew that Pelotti had been taken off the night train on his instructions, but all he said was: 'It is true that I received an anonymous telephone call to say that Pelotti would be on the train, but it was not from Charvet. It was a woman's voice.'

Less than an hour after he left Courtrand, Gautier was driving through Place Vendôme with Clémentine Lyse. He had received a message from her asking him to meet her at her couturiers in Rue de la Paix and when he arrived there she had been waiting for him in her carriage. She was looking as attractive as he had ever seen her, in a pale blue dress and a hat decorated with a blue ostrich feather and carrying a pink parasol. The victoria in which they rode was upholstered in royal blue and the coachman was dressed in pale blue livery and royal blue top hat and boots. When Gautier climbed into the carriage next to her, she gave no explanation as to why she had sent for him, but called out to the coachman to start. One could tell from the way in which she held her head and the expressive movements of her hands that she was in excellent spirits.

'I conclude that you have solved all your puzzles,' she told him as the carriage moved off. 'Or otherwise you would not have time to spend with me in mid-morning.'

'Yes, the Monterant affair is over as far as I am concerned.'

'And what have you learned since I saw you last?'

'Only that Sophie Monterant died by mischance. The poisoned chocolates were intended for Françoise.'

'For Françoise?' The idea seemed to amuse Clémentine. 'So Sophie's final rôle was that of understudy? She would have hated that!'

They drove through the Place de la Concorde and up towards Etoile. On the right of the Avenue des Champs-Elysées children were playing on the lawns in front of the Alcazar d'Eté and the Théâtre Marigny. It was a favoured place for the governesses of society families to take their charges in the mornings. Boys in sailor suits were playing prisoner's base among the laurels while little girls, their long hair hanging down, bowled their hoops past the little wooden booths from which, if they were good, their German or English governesses would allow them to buy toys or ginger-bread or barley sugar.

'I'm to give a special performance at the Eldorado tonight,' Clémentine told Gautier. 'The stage is to be decorated with hundreds of flowers in my honour and after my last song rose-petals will be released to float down from the ceiling.'

'Is that by way of an apology on the part of the management?'

'Yes, and from my admirers. At L'Attentat too there will be a celebration for my return. What form it will take I cannot say. It is to be a surprise.'

'I told you your public would wish to make up for the way they have treated you.'

'You were right,' she said and laughed happily.

From Etoile they drove down the Avenue du Bois towards the Bois-de-Boulogne. As they were passing the Comte de Limousin's house, the comtesse rode out in the avenue on a magnificent black horse, accompanied by her beautiful secretary, who was mounted on a white Arab mare. The comtesse was dressed not in the customary woman's riding habit but in the breeches and riding coat of a man. She was not the first woman in Paris to defy convention in this way and it was a style affected by a whole clique of Amazons for their daily ride in the Bois. As their carriage passed the two riders, Clémentine turned and inclined her head towards the comtesse, who acknowledged her greeting by raising her riding crop in a masculine salute.

'As we are going to the Bois,' Gautier said, 'could I take the liberty of inviting you to lunch with me there?'

There were several restaurants to be found in the Bois, some of them popular with the gratin, like the Cascade and the Pavillon d'Armenonville where the Prince of Wales, before he became King of England, often used to dine after an afternoon's racing. A meal at either would have cost the equivalent of at least a month's salary, but Gautier had an impulse to make a reckless gesture, not because he wished to impress Clémentine nor because he was seduced by the splendour and style of the beautiful women and the cavaliers whom they passed riding in the sunshine of a beautiful day, but as a response to the frustration which had been nagging at him ever since he had left Courtrand's office, frustration at knowing that the wrong man was going to the guillotine and that he could do nothing about it.

'I'm sorry, Jean-Paul,' Clémentine replied, 'but I have already accepted an invitation to lunch.'

'As usual I'm too late,' Gautier said flippantly to conceal his disappointment. 'Some other day then?'

As they drove past the Pavillon de Bagatelle, once the home of the Comte d'Artois, which had then passed to Sir Richard Wallace, the natural son of an English milord, Clémentine was silent, as though preoccupied with a problem which she had no wish to share with Gautier.

Suddenly she said, 'I'm lunching at Ledoyen with General Jacques Lafitte. We had dinner together last night as well at the Grand Véfour. That's the reason I wished to speak to you today.'

Gautier made no comment. Although he guessed what Clémentine was trying to say and knew he had no wish to hear it, part of himself remained detached and observed with amusement how maladroitly she had expressed herself. She continued: 'Please don't think that I am hard and unfeeling, Jean-Paul. I shall always be grateful to you because you taught me so much about myself, but with Jacques it is different. He has no one. He needs me.'

'Of course. I understand.'

'Do you know?' She could not conceal her delight at what she had to tell him. 'He has been invited to the gala at the Opéra in honour of the shah and wished to take me as his partner. But of course, it's impossible. He cannot go as long as he is in mourning for his wife.'

As he crossed the Seine from the Ile de la Cité to the Left Bank, Gautier tried to analyse his feelings for Clémentine. He recognized the finality of what she had said to him an hour earlier. Without intending to, she had made it clear, not that another man had supplanted him in her life, but that she had never had any affection, nor even any real interest in him. For a few hours, while they had been together, he had supposed that the death of Sophie

Monterant had released Clémentine from an obsession and released too her innate qualities of sincerity and sympathy and even humility. Now he realized without bitterness that their relationship had been only an interlude, like a brief period of sobriety in a drunkard's life, before she continued her quest for professional success and social acceptance.

When he reached the Café Corneille, Duthrey was already seated at their usual table, with a glass of port in front of him, reading a copy of his own newspaper. Seeing Gautier coming towards him, he folded the paper, took off the pince-nez which he wore for reading and put them into their case.

'It would appear that your problems in the Monterant affair have been resolved,' he said and then, tapping the newspaper with his finger, he added: 'We have published the story of Pelotti's confession.'

'Yes, it's almost an anticlimax, is it not?'

'How did you find out he was involved?'

'By luck. On an impulse I showed his photograph to Monterant's concierge and she identified him as the one who delivered the chocolates.'

'But why did he do it?'

'Because he was paid a large sum of money.'

'I see.' Duthrey did not ask who had paid Pelotti. It had long been an unspoken understanding that he would not take advantage of their friendship by asking for information on police matters which Gautier had not chosen to volunteer.

'If I gave you the name, you dare not publish it.'

'From the way you speak one senses that a man of some importance is involved.'

'A personage of importance, yes,' Gautier agreed. 'But it could equally well have been a woman.'

'Ah! So even if she were put on trial, she could plead a crime of passion and be acquitted.'

Juries in France were very susceptible to the defence of a 'crime passionel'. At a time when a woman had few rights and even less equality, almost the only place in which she stood at any advantage over a man was in the dock. Any woman of looks or intelligence or respectability could win a jury's sympathy, whatever her offence.

If she could plead that she had committed her crime to protect her marriage or her family, she was certain of an acquittal.

'This one will never be put on trial,' Gautier remarked.

'Is that because she has too much influence with the Sûreté?' Duthrey asked. He knew that such things had happened before in France.

'Not at all.' Gautier wished at least to give Courtrand the benefit of the doubt. Perhaps the Director-General would have pressed the case against the Charvets if the evidence had been stronger. 'Ironically the person responsible is only being sheltered from justice because Pelotti, a scoundrel who lived on women and was not above blackmail, will not betray a confederate.'

'Even so,' Duthrey said to console him, 'it must be satisfying to know you have solved a difficult case.'

'Scarcely that; if I had used my powers of logical thought a little sooner, at least one other person might not have died.'

He was thinking of both Madame Lafitte and Françoise, but before he could explain what he meant, a waiter came up to their table and handed Duthrey an envelope which had just been delivered at the café from *Figaro*. As he watched the journalist open the packet, Gautier remembered that it was a message from *Figaro* delivered to another café which had brought them the news of Sophie Monterant's death and he wondered at the coincidence.

When he had finished reading what was in the envelope, Duthrey said: 'My chief editor wants my advice.'

'Oh, yes?'

'We have been sent some documents anonymously and he is asking my opinion on whether we should publish what they contain.'

He passed over the envelope and a flash of intuition told Gautier what it must contain even before he began to pull out the bundle of letters and the photograph. He would in any case have recognized Adèle Charvet's flamboyant handwriting without re-reading the notes she had written to Pelotti or looking at her likeness in the autographed photograph.

'It is not the policy of *Figaro*,' Duthrey was saying, 'to publish scandal for the sake of scandal. Why should a man's career or a woman's life be ruined for a harmless indiscretion? On the other

175

hand, if they deserve to be exposed . . .' He left the sentence unfinished and spread his hands expressively.

'And what would happen if you published these?'

'The husband would be disgraced, his career at an end and the woman ostracized in society. Surely you remember the Antoine affair?'

Duthrey was referring to André Antoine, a radical agitator who had been guillotined for assassinating a judge and who, like Pelotti, was known to be a lover of renown. When he was arrested, compromising letters from the wife of René Gilbert, the editor of a liberal newspaper, had been found in Antoine's possession. Gilbert, in keeping with his liberal views, had decided to forgive his wife and to stand by her. Soon after Antoine had been executed, Gilbert and his wife were leaving the theatre after a gala charity performance and as they appeared at the entrance a wag in the crowd who had gathered to see the celebrities called out: 'Fetch the carriage of the Widow Antoine!' The remark, reprinted gleefully by the press, triggered off a campaign of ridicule which made the lives of the wretched Gilberts so unbearable that they were forced to leave France.

Gautier spread Adèle Charvet's letters out on the table and said to Duthrey, choosing his words with care: 'Disgrace? Humiliation? If you are asking my opinion, I believe that this woman and her husband deserve nothing less.'

'You have no idea of who might have sent us these letters, I suppose?'

'It wasn't me, if that's what you're thinking. The last time I saw these letters and the photograph, they were in the private safe of a very senior official at the Sûreté.'

Duthrey exploded with laughter as he realized the implications of Gautier's words. 'Well, old friend, that must prove something.'

'Yes. It proves that Cros was wrong. Neither justice nor the Sûreté, it seems, is blindfolded.'